The Minorities

THE PILOT

TERRI CELESTINE BRUNSON

Order this book online at www.trafford.com
or email orders@trafford.com

Most Trafford titles are also available at major online book retailers.

Print information available on the last page.

ISBN: 978-1-4907-7122-9 (sc)
ISBN: 978-1-4907-7130-4 (e)

Trafford rev. 06/08/2016

 www.trafford.com

North America & international
toll-free: 1 888 232 4444 (USA & Canada)
fax: 812 355 4082

Table of Contents

Dedication

"The Minorities, The Pilot" is dedicated to
all battered women worldwide.

Also I dedicate "The Minorities" to my family

Wesley Brunson Sr.
Wesley Jr. and Neyome Sathyseelan-Brunson
The Sathyseelan family
Ruth Ann Brunson

Lorenzo Mitchell Sr.

Sherri Celestine Brunson Mitchell
Lorenzo Denarde Mitchell Jr. Octavia and
Chris Smalls Justin Jamal Mitchell Sr.
Great Nieces Ta'neisha
Keeley Mitchell, Laila Smalls and Triniti Jordan Osborne
Great Nephews Christian Alexander Smalls and Justin Jamal Jr.
Myself, Ms. Terri Celestine
Brunson
My SonZachary Nicholas Sheals
And to my love, Dameyon M. Harrell

Chapter One

"Your Secret Is Safe with Me"

It was the early morning at the Wilkerson Household. Emily Wilkerson was briefly alerted by her alarm clock before she was awakened to a typical good morning. She turned over in her bed onto her back, facing up at the ceiling. She muffled under her voice as she awakened.

"Oh my God...tell me it isn't morning already!"

Her mother, Judith Wilkerson was at the end of the staircase yelling up to Emily to come down for breakfast before it got cold.

"Get ready Emily, come on downstairs for breakfast, you too, Daniel."

Daniel was ready for the morning. He couldn't resist smelling the aroma of a good breakfast. It was top priority for him, because he thought it would improve his brain cells and his way of thinking. Daniel came downstairs to the aroma of breakfast cookin, it hit his nose very hard.

"Oh mama that smells so wonderful...good ole bacon... sausage...eggs... toast...every young man's dream to have good sustenance!"

Donnie, Judith's husband, followed behind Daniel. He put on his coat preparing himself for a quick breakfast before he had to leave for work.

"Hey baby...is everything ready? I got to be out the door in thirty minutes, so I'll be on the road to work on time."

"Donnie...breakfast is almost ready. Here is your heaping cup of coffee to start off the morning. You better go ahead and drink it while it's hot while I get your breakfast. I'll put more in your thermos."

"Baby...I put plenty of coffee in that thermos, because I feel that it will be a long day for me." Donnie said while he sat at the head of the table, waiting for breakfast to be served.

"Don't I always put enough coffee in your thermos, Donnie? Breakfast will be ready in a minute", Judith replied while preparing the breakfast.

Emily came downstairs into the kitchen. She prepared to leave before she could have breakfast with her family. Sarah Langston, Emily's best friend had something personal she wanted to discuss with her.

"Hey, mama, I got to leave a little early this morning. I got to meet with Sarah. She has something she wants to tell me."

Judith was a concerned mother for her daughter, Emily. She was determined to find out what was so important that her friend Sarah Langston had to tell her before she left in a rush out the door without eating a good breakfast. It was Judith's way of expressing to Emily that eating a good breakfast will improve her way of thinking in the morning.

"Is Sarah okay, Emily? I mean...what is so important what Sarah have to tell you that you must rush off before you eat a good breakfast?" Judith questioned Emily while she packed her book bag with her school books.

"Nothing to worry about, mama…I'm going to grab a piece of toast and go. See you later on today…mama, daddy." Emily replied.

Emily grabbed a piece of toast and rushed out the front door without leaving a trace of anything else but a trail of bread crumbs. Judith was determined to know what the secret was between her daughter and her best friend Sarah…the secret they was keeping so privately to themselves. Judith looked over at Donnie as she watched Emily walk out the front door.

"What was that all about, Donnie? What was so important that Emily had to rush out of this house so early is what I want to know? As a matter of fact, Emily has been leaving early every day for the past three mornings. I really don't like it when she leaves without eating a good breakfast. She's already too thin for me as it is."

"I don't know, Judith! I really don't know what's in those girls minds these days. It's like a privacy sector if you ask me. Everything is a secret!"

Daniel used Emily as an example, unlikely, when most brothers aggravate their sisters in order to get their point across. It gave Daniel a motive to constantly pick on his sister, Emily.

"Tell me about it daddy! Take Emily for an example. She has briefly lost her mind about a lot of things.

This secret thing, private sector, or whatever, or however you want to say it, just happened a few days ago. Daddy, I really want to help my sister with her problem. She goes out of the house without feeding her face, but in a whole lot of ways, I love her. I'm her brother. That's how I show her that I love her…when I pick at her… at least that's my prospective of things." Daniel said in concern for his sister, Emily.

"Here's something I can tell you Daniel. Your sister hasn't lost her mind and I love her just the way she is. That's my prospective of things,"

Judith sets the table for breakfast very neatly with all the trimmings. She placed a platter of bacon, sausage, scrambled eggs onto the table. She also brought a platter of toast all lined up like a bunch of fallen dominos. There were buttery spreads, homemade jellies and jams centered neatly in the middle of the table for everyone to get whatever they wanted to eat. Judith turned to Daniel. She chastised him with for picking at his sister.

"Daniel, I want you to leave your sister alone this second. Breakfast is served gentlemen. Let's eat!"

Donnie began to fill his plate with everything from each platter of breakfast food.

"Baby, this looks and smells good if I do say so myself!"

Judith briefly glanced up at the clock. She saw that time was passing by for Donnie to leave for work.

She suggested that Donnie hurry, before he was too late getting out the door.

"Sweetheart, you better get ready and go ahead out of the door. You only got twenty-five minutes left until you got to be at work."

Daniel decided to inform his mother and father about going over to his best friend Reginald's house instead of coming straight home from school to do his homework, chores and read a book of his choosing–things that an average teen would get out of doing.

"Hey mama, daddy, Reginald wants me to come over to his house after school. Can I go…please?"

Daniel continued begging his parents permission to go straight to his best friend, Reginald's house after school. As any parent would do when their child asks a question—like, "Can I go to my friend's house after school."—Donnie and Judith were very direct with their answer to Daniel's question.

"Daniel, you know that I'm your father and I love you, but you know the rules and regulations around this house. Listen to what I'm about to say to you...you know that you got homework. You know that you need to come straight home and do your homework before you do anything else. So you know I don't need to say anything more; you know my answer to your question." Donnie discreetly answered Daniel's question...breaking it down to him.

"Daniel...you know that I'm your mother and I love you as well, but like your father said, you know the rules and regulations of this house. You need to come straight home from school and do your homework. You really need to clean that pig sty of a room and nothing else. I don't need to say anything more; you also know my answer to your question."

Judith discreetly answered Daniel's question and also breaking it down to him.

Daniel came back at his parents with total disrespect. He smart-mouth his parents...which in terms...considered him very uncaring to his parents when they tried to help him to be responsible for things like doing his homework, chores, or maybe reading a book. Something that would help in the long run...once he's out in the world to live on his own.,

"Okay, whatever! You hardly let me go anyways!"

Donnie got ready to leave for work. He packed up the rest of his breakfast in a paper napkin. He leaned over and gave Judith a kiss before leaving for work.

"Hey babe...I'm taking the rest of my breakfast with me. See you later on today." Donnie said as he quickly started out the door. "Donnie, here's your thermos!" Judith yelled out to Donnie. "Please baby...have a wonderful day today and be careful...love you." Donnie rushed out the front door with the rest of his breakfast in a napkin in one hand; his lunch pail in the other hand.

"See you later, babe! I'll be careful...love you too."

Judith gathered Daniel's school supplies and placed them in his backpack. She glanced over at Daniel eating his breakfast.

"Daniel...finish your breakfast, the bus will be coming for you in ten minutes."

After Judith gathered all Daniel's school supplies to put in his backpack, she cleared the breakfast dishes from the table. She proceeded to start lunch for later on during the day.

Meanwhile at Middleton High, where Emily and Sarah attended. Sarah was very emotional. She mopped around pacing back and forth on the school's courtyard. She was met by Emily coming out the back entrance of the school and onto the courtyard.

"Emily…I don't know what to do about my situation. I'm totally scared and confused." Sarah frantically cried out to Emily as they continued to pace the courtyard.

"Sarah…did you tell your mama about your pregnancy yet?" Emily questioned Sarah.

"No…I can't tell her that, Emily! There is so much chaos going on at my house right now. I defiantly can't put my pregnancy on top what's going at my house." Sarah replied in fear.

"Okay…whatever, Sarah!" What about that creep Richard Morris? He is the father of your baby? What is he saying about this, or is he going to do anything about it?" Emily questioned Sarah with concern for her well-being.

"Richard is doing what almost every guy would do when girl get pregnant. Nothing! He's not helping me decide what we should do before the baby comes. He's not saying anything to me that's worth hearing."

Emily and Sarah briefly interrupted each other backwards and forwards about the facts of an ongoing problem with teenage pregnancies and about guys who want help coparent. The girls acknowledged their concerns about teenage pregnancies as they spoke amongst themselves about the issues intact.

"Sarah…I just don't understand! Some of these guys; they do nothing to help with the situation in hand. First, they get with you and then, they whisper sweet nothings to you; they draw you into their web of deceit, and then, Sarah, they have you where they want you and leave you when they find out there's a little bun in the oven. At least most of these guys to when they find out you're pregnant." Emily briefly outlined to Sarah about the realities of a deceitful man.

"Emily…I feel so alone! I was drawn in Richard's web. He did what he wanted with me. I let him have me and now… I have this precious little bun growing inside me. Sometimes I don't know whether I'm excited, or if it's the end of the world for me." Sarah said with emotion.

"It's not the end of the world for you, Sarah. I tell you what… why don't you come over to my house for a few hours, take a load off until you decide what you're going to do."

"Emily, I sure can use the break from all of the things going on in my life right now. It's better than going home and facing up to the chaos and with my mother flying off the deep handle over this. My dad is very cool everything, but I wonder what he's going to do when I tell him about my pregnancy. I hope he takes this news without taking my head off. I would hate to see him fly off the deep handle like my mother would."

Emily and Sarah proceeded towards the back door entrance of the school from the courtyard. They went to their lockers to grab their books that they needed for their classes.

"Sarah…meet me here at the lockers after school today." Emily said before she went to her first class.

"We'll walk to my house afterwards."

"Okay Emily! Thanks for just being a friend and being here for me. I'll meet you here at the lockers after classes today. See you later, Emily. Thanks for being my friend." Sarah said after she grabbed her books from her locker.

"What are friends for, Sarah! See you right here at the lockers… don't forget."

Emily and Sarah went their separate ways to their classes. The school hallways filled up with students, faculties' members, and other sources on their way to their class.

Chapter Two

"Sarah's Secret Revealed"

It was early in the afternoon at the Wilkerson Household. The phone rang. Judith picked up. Donnie was on the receiving end of the phone at his job. Judith received Donnie's call.

"Hello Donnie! What's up sweetie? What! How long are you're going to be this afternoon? Okay…see you when you arrive home. Bye!"

Judith's friend, Lisa Powers came over for a visit and a conversation. Lisa knocked at the back door.

After her call with Donnie, Judith hanged up the phone quickly. She signaled for Lisa by waving her hand for her to come in. "Knock…knock…Judith! Can I come in please?" Judith replied.

"Come in Lisa. How are you?"

"I'm fine! How are you, Judith?"

"Fine! I can't complain, Lisa. Donnie got to work over a little bit today a work. Would you like a cold glass of iced tea, Lisa?" Judith offered Lisa.

"Yes! I don't mind if I do, Judith. Thanks. So…Donnie got to work over? Overtime is good! It means you can have the extra things that you need here and for the family." Lisa said.

"Yes Lisa and that's the best thing about my Donnie working over is that we're getting the extra things that we do need here and for our family." Judith replied.

"Judith…. it's been kind of hard on me and my family, since I got laid off at the office three weeks ago."

Lisa said with disappointment.

"What happened at the office, Lisa?" Judith questioned Lisa with concern.

"I guess the way the economy is right now and with no money rolling through the company, it's not enough money and resources to keep the company afloat, or anything else in that matter." Lisa responded with concern about how she was going to help her husband take care of their home without financial support.

Judith and Lisa proceeded into the living room with their cold glasses of iced teas to continue their conversation on the sofa.

"I guess I can be thankful for Donnie. Judith said with appreciation for Donnie. "Getting a little overtime does come in handy. With Donnie being the only one working and the way he feels about me working; he says he makes enough for the both of us. I still feel I should contribute to the household too."

"I guess so, Judith. That's your opinion! For me…it's different. I know I got to find another job somewhere. I don't know what I'm going to do. Oh well!" Lisa said as she gave a difference in opinion when it comes to having a job and helping with the finances in her household.

"Just like you said…this is a poor economy and jobs are scarce these days. You'll manage, Lisa. You will! Judith assured Lisa that the grass will be greener for her…job wise.

"I know I will, Judith. So tell me…how is your daughter Emily and your son Daniel? Lisa questioned Judith. "I don't see much of them these days."

"They're peddling around with their friends mostly." Judith replied as a mother concerned for her daughter. "Emily raced out of here like her whole tail was on fire very early this morning without eating a good breakfast. She just grabbed a piece of toast and rushed out the front door. Emily said that it was something her friend Sarah Langston had to tell her at school. Lisa…I'm so determined to know what was so important that Emily had to rush out of the house like she did this morning. This secret Sarah had to tell Emily…I really hope nothing is wrong with Sarah, or Emily if I have anything else to say about what their so secretive about. I guess it's none of my business, or should I make it my business…especially when it comes to my teenage daughter."

"I feel that it is your business…especially where your daughter is concerned. I'm quite sure Emily isn't going to tell you what's going on with her, or about Sarah in the matter both girls being so secretive, Judith. Maybe…just maybe in due time Emily or Sarah or both girls will fess up in the meantime." Lisa replied to Judith about the realities of the private sector where secrets are kept safe and soundless.

"I'm sure it's something very important, but very disturbing. I don't know! Donnie told me, it's like a privacy sector some of these girls and boys display when everything is a secret. I that's teenagers. We were teens once. I hope it's nothing extremely serious, Lisa!" Judith said with extreme concern for her daughter Emily.

Lisa was curious and very concerned for Emily and her friend Sarah and why they were being so secretive. She pinpointed Judith's concern for her daughter, Emily. Lisa really wanted to get to meat of what of Emily's and Sarah's secret was about. Lisa and Judith was very noisy to the point of no return.

They were determined to break the privacy sector of Emily's and Sarah's secret. They began conversing briefly about what was going on with the girls.

"Judith…do you think something bad about what is going on with Emily and Sarah that we both should know about…I mean in Emily's case…being that she is your daughter?" Lisa questioned Judith putting Emily and Sarah's secret under investigation.

"I don't think so, Lisa! I really don't think so. Maybe we're reading too much into this secret. Emily and Sarah do have a right to their privacy." Judith said.

Judith and Lisa sat on the sofa with their cold glasses iced teas in their hands. They stared at each other, thinking that maybe something more was going on with Emily and Sarah than they were letting on. Judith was still very determined to find out what the secret was between Emily and Sarah, even if it's was a teen thing.

It was 2:30 p.m. in the afternoon when school let out. Emily and Sarah was walking home from the school. Sarah became emotional again about her pregnancy. She confided in Emily in order to help her get through her trials and tribulations of her unplanned pregnancy.

"Emily…how can I be so stupid is to let myself get pregnant?" Sarah cried out.

"Sarah…you're not stupid and you didn't do this by yourself. Emily said as a reminder to Sarah that it takes two to create another life beyond her own. "I don't know what it's like to be in your position Sarah, but I will tell you…with support of your dad, my mom, or maybe my father, I sure things will work out for you, Sarah." Emily said.

"Emily…how is that possible?" Sarah replied with slight haste. "Who's going to help me out? — I know Richard Morris isn't going to lift a finger to me raise our child. He's too busy running around trying to be a pimp…running around with his bum friends, doing nothing but being acting silly."

"Sarah…Please…never depend on a guy if he's not going to be a man for and about taking care of his responsibility, or being there for you and your child." Emily replied to Sarah as they walked closer to home.

Still feeling depressed, Sarah took what Emily said to her into complete consideration. She had thoughts about her boyfriend, Richard Morris. She had hoped he would change his tune about being there...at least for their unborn child.

"I know what you're saying, Emily. It's just that...I wish Richard would grow up and be a man enough to take on the responsibility as a soon to be father...at least for our unborn child's sake. That's all!"

"He's not, Sarah!" Emily replied to Sarah about Richard for not being a responsible for his part in their situation and Sarah's pregnancy. "Richard is not going to be responsible. Look what he's doing to you! I heard...and this is just a rumor, Sarah. I heard that he does not even claim he's the father."

Sarah was startled about Emily's comment about Richard. He claimed not to be the father of her unborn child.

"Emily...he's going around saying that he doesn't claim the baby. Are you serious! He doesn't claim the baby!

"That's the rumor, Sarah. Come on...get over him, Sarah. Please...stop making it seem like you can't do without this creep... like this baby is going to keep you both together. Having a baby isn't going to make Richard be closer to you or you baby. He doesn't care, Sarah! My God...get over him...please!" Emily said in great concern for Sarah's pride and dignity. "You're right, Emily. I got to stop feeling sorry for myself and stop using the baby to make Richard see me, or help me take care of the baby, because...he isn't like you said he wouldn't. Sarah decided to put the issue of her pregnancy to rest where Richard was concerned. "I'm going to do what I need to do for me and for my child. I think I better tell my parents."

"That's a start, Sarah. So...let's stop thinking or talking about this for a while. Let's get to my house and drown ourselves in a hot fudge sundae as Emily and Sarah had arrived to Emily's house. They went inside the house straight to the kitchen to make their hot fudge sundaes. Emily and Sarah ate their sundaes without mentioning anything about pregnancies, or about Richard being responsible. Meanwhile...at Lenard's Frozen Food Factory, Donnie's place of employment. Donnie had finished a late shift with overtime included. He clocked out as he left the facility. Outside...Donnie was met by his coworker and best friend, Stanley Powers.

"My Lord, Stan...I'm tired!" Donnie walked out of factory barely picking up his arms and feet off the ground, because he was so tired. "My Lord...it seems like I've been on my job ever since yesterday afternoon, but I say...I'm very happy about getting some overtime for a change and it's just in time too. I got a lot of things to do and take care of at home." Donnie said barely keeping his eyes open from tiredness.

"I understand what you're talking about, Donnie." Stanley replied. "My wife, Lisa...she lost her job at the office about three weeks ago and it's really been hard on her, and it's been a strain on our financial situation...you know...bills and such." Stanley revealed to Donnie about his wife losing her job.

"Stan...I've been there in that same situation more than once... more than twice. I do make enough money, so Judith can stay home, but...she wants to work, just in case my overtime stops." Donnie expressed to Stanley about Judith's determination to help Donnie support their family.

"With the way things are going with the economy...people losing their jobs every single day. Jobs are hard to come by." The reality is that you need both parties working in order to hold a household Donnie and Stanley were met by another one of their coworkers, Paul Langston...Sarah's father. He walked around to where Stanley and Donnie was in the parking lot as they approached their cars.

"Hello Don...Stan...how's it going today?" Paul greeted Stanley and Donnie. "Yeah, I tell you...every single day we work overtime is a blessing to me and for my daughter, Sarah. I'm not so sure what my wife thinks about anything I do, or if she cares at all when I bring home the bacon. She's so busy doing her thing out in the street. God only knows what she does with her time. I feel so bad for my daughter, Sarah. She's walking around like she's lost in another world. She's not talking to me about anything. Everything is a secret where Sarah is concerned."

"My Lord, Paul…that's deep. I feel the same about my daughter, Emily. Secrets! Judith and I have that same problem with Emily. What are you going to do about your daughter, Sarah Paul?" Donnie shared the same privacy sector with Paul when it came to entering their girl's privacy sector.

"I don't know, Donnie! I hope nothing serious is wrong with Sarah. I'm not going to put too much into this, but…I feel something really is going on with Sarah. I haven't pin pointed the problem. Sarah will not talk to me about anything. I feel my daughter is shutting me out!" Paul was very concerned for his daughter Sarah. "Donnie…maybe it's a woman thing." Donnie replied to Paul. "Most daddy's girls like to communicate with their daddies, some don't.

I wish my daughter, Emily would tell me what's on her mind, but I know I can't force her to do so. She doesn't want her daddy prying into her business. You know how that is."

Paul was very disgusted with Sarah's mother, Susan and how she carried herself as a very disrespectful woman when it comes to being a mother to Sarah. "That's my point, Stan! Sarah doesn't have a mother to influence her, or direct her in the right way and put her in a good state of mind on some of the woman issues that I really can't help her with."

"My daughter, Emily, is her best friend, Paul. They've been talking a lot lately. My daughter rushed out of the house this morning. She said Sarah had something she wanted to tell her. I don't know what that is." Donnie said.

"Maybe Donnie…your wife can talk to Sarah; being that she needs a mother figure in her life. That's if Sarah decides to open that door on what she's being secretive about like teenage girls normally are."

Paul gives Donnie's wife Judith permission to talk to and question Sarah about what's been going on with her.

"Donnie…Paul…I'll see you both tomorrow morning at work."

Stanley proceeded in a different location of the parking lot where his car was parked. Donnie came upon his car. He got into his car.

"I'll talk to my wife about Sarah, Paul. That's if Sarah is up to spilling the beans. Maybe she'll talk with Judith about her problem…if you don't mind, Paul…do you?" Donnie said. Paul belittled his wife, Susan to Donnie about her motherly position.

"I really don't have a choice in this matter with my Sarah, Donnie…like I said, her mother is a lost cause in the matter of our daughter, Sarah. Maybe your wife, Judith, will can get Sarah to talk about what's on her mind."

"Okay…I let you know tomorrow, Paul. Bring her over tonight." Donnie replied.

"Oh…I forgot to tell you, Donnie, Sarah called me earlier from school today. She walked home with your daughter, Emily from school today." Paul pulled his keys out of his pocket. Donnie cranked his car. He was ready to leave Lenard's Frozen Food Facility. Donnie turned to Paul while placing his car into gear to back out of the parking lot.

"Okay, that's great, Paul. Tonight…Judith can talk to Sarah today what's been going on with her. Just maybe she can see if she can figure out what's been on her mind lately, or to see if she has any issues I need to know about. I'll bring her home later on tonight, if you don't mind, Paul." Paul thanked Donnie.

"Thanks for what your wife, Judith is doing for Sarah. She is what's right for my daughter, when it comes to giving motherly advice.

Donnie drove off towards home while Paul looked on with curiosity of his daughter's secrecy and her intuitions.

It was the late afternoon at the Wilkerson's household. Judith served dinner with Sarah in attendance.

Daniel wondered about his father's absence at the dinner table. He questioned his mother about why he was always coming home late from work.

"Mama…where's daddy? He was supposed to be home hours ago?"

"Daniel…your father will be home in a little while. He had to work overtime today so that we will have everything we need and for our house." Judith replied to Daniel's question about his father's absence at the dinner table.

"Oh…I guess that's okay, mama." Daniel continue to eat his dinner.

Emily became offensive towards Daniel for not caring, or appreciating what their father did for the family and the house. She started to belittle Daniel about the questions he asked about their dad's absence from the dinner table. Emily started calling him names. "No Daniel…you numb head…that's great! Our father works overtime so we can have everything that we need for the house and for us. Don't you get it you block head?"

Daniel took offence to Emily's remarks and for calling him a numb head and a block head in front of her friend, Sarah. He returned the favor to Emily right in front of her friend Sarah by offering her the same fate, but with more haste. "Well, excuse me you numb skull! Why don't you go somewhere and hide under a rock! Just maybe I'll forget that you're hiding under there and I won't come looking for you."

Sarah was in disbelief from the insults made from Emily and Daniel as they continued to insult each other in haste.

"You all are crazy!" Judith shouted out.

Judith demanded that Emily apologize to her brother for starting the name calling and disrespecting him in front of her friend, Sarah at the dinner table.

"Emily, you know you're wrong! You started the name calling and I want you to apologize right now to your brother for disrespecting him in front of your friend.

Do it now!"

Emily apologized to Daniel.

"I'm sorry for calling you a numb head…even though…."

"Emily...stop it!" Judith said. "Okay, mama! I'm sorry, Daniel... really!"

"Apology accepted," Daniel responded as he accepted his sister partially genuine apology.

Judith sat down to the dinner table and ate dinner with her children...with Sarah in attendance. She immediately initiated a conversation with Sarah in order to get her to talk about any issues she had, or any problems she's coping with.

"So Sarah...what's been going on with you lately? The way Emily stormed out of here very early this morning, it must have been something really very important? She questioned Sarah. She said that you had something to tell her, but I don't want to pry into your business dear. I'm very concerned about you. I'm not your mother, but...would like to help if I can, or if you let me."

"Oh...it's nothing, Mrs. Wilkerson. You don't need to bother yourself with my problems." Sarah replied to Judith with her secret still bound in her heart in soul.

Emily interrupted her mother.

"Oh, mom...don't worry...everything is fine!" Emily tried to keep Sarah from spilling the bean about her pregnancy.

"Don't interrupt, Emily! Now Sarah...how is your mother?" Judith asked Sarah.

"Mrs. Wilkerson.... it's hard to say sometimes. It's like...I hardly see her sometimes. She's out all times of the night and comes home whenever she ready to come home. She claims to work late and the majority of the time, I don't believe it."

Donnie came home surprisingly from a long day at work. He came in through the front door quietly. He wanted to surprise his family. Donnie proceeded into the dining room where Judith, Emily, Daniel, and Sarah were at the dinner table. Donnie talked to Sarah about her father and their family issues. Donnie decided to take the matter into consideration and talk with Sarah.

"How's everyone doing tonight?" Judith answered Donnie.

"We're doing fine babe.

How was your day at work? I see you've made a lot of overtime today?" Judith responded.

Donnie leaned down and kissed Judith on the lips.

"It was hard, but it was worth the effort. I made to get those extra hours in order for us to be able to afford the things we need for our house and for us."

Emily and Daniel were very excited about their father coming home early from work. They both greeted their father with open arms. Emily was really excited to see her father.

"Hello, daddy! How are you today? Daniel and I really miss having you here on time for dinner, but it's okay. I mean, with the overtime! It's worth it...because you are worth the excitement, so that my brother and I can continue to welcome you home."

Daniel walked over and shook hands with his father.

"Hello, pops! How art thou? I miss you...I mean...at the dinner table, but I understand the hard work and everything else you're doing for us. I'm very proud of you, pops!"

"Your dad love's you both. Hi Sarah...how are you doing?"

"I'm fine, Mr. Wilkerson." Sarah replied.

Donnie began to converse with Sarah about her father's concern for her wellbeing. Sarah abruptly reacted to Donnie's line of questioning about her about father and how worried he was about her.

"Sarah...your father is very worried about you." Donnie said.

"Is he okay, Mr. Wilkerson? Is he okay?" Sarah questioned Mr. Wilkerson.

Donnie assured Sarah that her father was okay.

"Yes Sarah...your father is fine. He's worried about you."

Sarah briefly glanced over at Emily...worried that her secret will be out, if the line of questioning continued.

"Mr. Wilkerson...why is my father worried about me?" Sarah asked Mr. Wilkerson.

Emily interrupted her father while questioning Sarah.

"Daddy...Sarah father is fine."

"Don't interrupt, Emily! Donnie replied only to keep Emily from interupting from questioning Sarah about the secret she's been keeping to herself. "Her dad says that there is something wrong with you Sarah. He decided that maybe this is a girl thing…a situation more in need of a woman's advice and attention. He says you don't talk to him about anything, and that he's worried about you…very worried Sarah."

Sarah became startled, because she knew she was being found out about her pregnancy. Sarah was reluctant to keep the news about her pregnancy a secret.

"It's nothing, Mr. Wilkerson. It's nothing! It's nothing!" Sarah hesitated to tell Mr. Wilkerson about her pregnancy.

"Okay Sarah…maybe I'll go ahead and leave for about ten minutes or so. I got to and take a shower anyways. Maybe you'll feel more comfortable without my presence. Judith…darling…put my dinner in the oven please…will you dear." Donnie signaled Judith with a wink to start a conversation with Sarah about her problem and the secret she was keeping between her and Emily.

"Okay baby." Judith said while signaling back to Donnie her pinky finger.

Judith prepared Donnie's dinner and placed it in the oven. Judith sat back at the dinner table with Sarah and her children. She was determined to get Sarah to talk about what been going on, so that her father wouldn't worry so much about her. Emily asked to be excused from the table…along with Sarah.

"Mom…can Sarah and I be excused so that we can go up upstairs to my room?"

"Not quite yet, girls." Judith replied. "I would like to talk to you, Sarah."

Sarah was concerned about what Mrs. Wilkerson had to say. Sarah was espcially reluctant to reveal her pregnancy to Mrs. Wilkerson. She continued to keep it a secret.

"What is this about, Mrs. Wilkerson?"

"Tell me, Sarah…baby! It's not hard to notice that something's with you."

Daniel abruptly interrupted his mother's and Sarah's conversation.

"Oh my God…Sarah! Are you and my sister are in trouble!" Judith turned to Daniel and demanded that he be quiet.

"Daniel hush! Take your plate. Get a dinner tray and go upstairs and finish your dinner, please? Thank your son. This is girl talk!" Daniel got up and left the dinner table. He retrieved a dinner tray out of the pantry to place his dinner plate on. Daniel proceeded upstairs to his room while muttering to Emily and Sarah.

"T-R-O-U-B-L-E!"

"Daniel go! Judith shouted towards the stairway at Daniel was muttering at Emily and Sarah

"Son…. go upstairs now" Daniel disappeared upstairs. Judith continued her conversation with Sarah.

"Now Sarah…like I said, it's not hard to notice that you have a problem. Emily rushed out of this house this morning without breakfast. I know at that moment that something wasn't right about what was going on between you two." Sarah assured Mrs. Wilkerson that nothing was wrong with her, or Emily.

"It's nothing, …Mrs. Wilkerson?

"Sarah…the way Emily has been storming out of this morning and every morning after that without eating a good breakfast, it was possible that something's not right here sweetie. Emily never spends time with the family anymore since this secret that you and Emily are holding on too."

Emily continued to take up for Sarah as she continued to be hesitant about concealing her secret to her mother, Judith. Judith began to worry about Sarah. She continued grilling Sarah.

"Mama…maybe I'm not hungry in the mornings."

"That's no excuse, Emily! Judith continued to grill Sarah. "I can't help but to be concerned about your wellbeing Sarah. What's going on my dear? Tell me, Sarah!" Sarah started crying…afraid that concealing her pregnancy will make matters for her.

"Well, Mrs. Wilkerson…I don't know if I can tell you, or anyone else but Emily." Sarah replied.

"How can anyone help you, Sarah, if you don't open up to me, or your father. Believe me Sarah…the look is there for anyone to notice that something isn't right with you. When you shut everyone out, and my daughter Emily is not there to help you, who are you going to call. Who is going to comfort you if you keep shutting everyone out.

Sarah glanced at Emily again.

Sarah began concealing her secret to Mrs. Wilkerson.

"I see your point! You're right, Mrs. Wilkerson, but…I don't think you can help me too much with this one."

"Try me, dear!" Judith challenged Sarah to reveal her secret.

Sarah finally put everyone's concerns about her to rest. She was still in tears as revealed her pregnancy to the Mrs. Wilkerson.

"Mrs. Wilkerson…I'm…I'm…I'm pregnant! I'm pregnant! I don't know what to do about it."

Judith wasn't surprised when Sarah revealed her pregnancy. In her heart, she knew it was possible that Sarah was indeed pregnant. Judith start grilling her Emily.

"Emily…how long you've known about this? I'm sure that Sarah told you…correct?"

"Yes…I've known all along." Emily replied to her mother truthfully about Sarah's pregnancy.

"Sarah…when was your last menstrual cycle?" Judith asked Sarah

"Almost three months ago, Mrs. Wilkerson." Sarah said abruptly.

Judith came up to Sarah and embraced her with motherly love. Sarah was deeply consumed deeply by Judith's motherly love towards her. Judith was Sarah's mother by heart. Judith convinced Sarah to tell her father about her pregnancy. Sarah became emotional once again about the possibility that her pregnancy that will either burden her father or in fact kill him.

"Your father need to be told about your pregnancy, Sarah." Judith said while embracing Sarah. Sarah cried fiercely in Judith's arms.

She trembled with fear that her father would be angry about her pregnancy.

"I can't tell him, Mrs. Wilkerson! I just can't tell my father about my pregnancy. This will kill him tremendously. With all the problems we already have at home, I can't put pregnancy on top of that!"

Sarah cried out to Judith. "I don't think so, Sarah!" Your father is very concerned. He loves you very much. He wants you to come to him when you have a problem...anytime. He wants to be involved in your life, Sarah." Judith assured Sarah about her father wanting to be involved in her troubles and her life.

As any young pregnant...scared teenager, Sarah was afraid about the possibility of being thrown out of her father's house if she discloses her pregnancy to him.

"Mrs. Wilkerson...what if my father kicks me out of the house?" Sarah said to Judith in fear of her father putting her on the street.

"Sarah...don't worry about that, he won't throw you out of the house. My husband and I will go ahead and take you home. We'll take it from there! Let's get your jacket. I'll call my husband downstairs, and we'll take you home. Just give us a minute."

Sarah and Emily were left alone as they conversed with one another.

Sarah and Emily were left alone as they conversed with one another. Emily anxiously questioned Sarah about revealing her pregnancy to her father.

"Well Sarah...what are you going to tell your dad?"

"I don't know what, or how to tell my dad this kind of news." Sarah responded. Emily comforted Sarah assuring her that her parents will be there for her whenever you have a problem.

"I guess with my parents there with you, Sarah, I think you'll be fine." Sarah build up the confidence to talk to her father about her pregnancy.

"I guess I got to get up the nerve to do so, Emily." Emily and Sarah shared an embrace.

"I guess that is what you have to do, Sarah. Give me a hug! I'm here for you, too."

Emily assured Sarah that everything would be okay before she left with her parents.

"Sarah...don't worry...get it over with and everything will be okay."

"Thanks for being there for me, Emily, I really appreciate your mama right now. She's just the mother figure I needed."

"No problem, Sarah! No problem! You're my best friend. I love you, girlfriend.

Don't you know that by now?"

"I do! I really know that you are the greatest friend I know from the bottom of my heart."

Donnie and Judith came downstairs. They were ready to take Sarah home. They proceeded towards the front door with Sarah. They got ready to exit. Donnie instructed Emily to take care of things while he and Judith and Sarah got ready to leave for the Langston household. Donnie opened the front door and held it like a gentleman. Both Judith and Sarah exited out the door.

"Emily...take care of the house while we're gone. Watch your brother as well, Emily, I mean it!"

Judith instructed Emily to babysit her brother while they were gone to the Langston household.

"Okay mama...daddy...I will do so! Sarah...see you in school tomorrow?"

Sarah turned back to Emily as she responded.

"Okay...thanks again for being there as my best friend."

Donnie, Judith, and Sarah exit the house down the walk way. They proceeded to get into the family car. Emily watched from the front door as her parents drove off with Sarah to the Langston household.

Chapter Three

"Daddy Understands"

It was the late evening. The Wilkerson's arrived at the Langston's household. Sarah was still very nervous about telling her father about her pregnancy. The Wilkerson's got out of the car and walked up to the front door. Sarah was reluctant to get out of the car.

"Mr. and Mrs. Wilkerson...I don't know about this. I'm very scared about what my father would do."

"Judith told me what happened, Sarah. Donnie said. I don't like the outcome of what happened to you, I will in fact support you with any decision you make about your pregnancy and I know your father will too."

Judith agreed with Donnie about Sarah's father. She knew that Paul would give full support to Sarah in any given situation with all the love that a father could give to his daughter, even if it's concerning his daughters pregnancy.

"Sarah...my husband is right! You know he's right about this."
Still Sarah was reluctant to tell her father about her pregnancy.

"Yes...but I'm scared Mrs. Wilkerson!"

"That's all into realizing all the reality of life. Obstacles are thrown at you. It's according to how you take them in...whether if it's by mind or the heart."

Donnie interrupted Judith.

"You learn to accept what obstacles are thrown at you and learn to be responsible for the many things that you're going through in your life. This is one of your reality checks. Accept it and be responsible Sarah."

Judith interrupted Donnie in return.

"Everything will be alright! Whatever you decide to do about your situation." Sarah got out of the car.

Donnie and Judith embraced Sarah while walking up to the front door. Sarah thanked the Wilkerson's for supporting her situation with her pregnancy.

"Thank you both! Emily is a very blessed and lucky to have you as parents. I'm lucky to have my father in my life. My mother...I don't know! I never know where she is!"

Donnie encouraged Sarah, knowing that she was still very nervous about concealing the news about her pregnancy to her father.

"Now...let's go and tell your father Sarah, shall we." Sarah smiled.

"We shall, Mr. Wilkerson. Let's get this over with."

Sarah knocked. Her father, Paul opened the front door. He was met by his daughter, Sarah and the Wilkerson's at the entrance of his door. Paul escorted the Wilkerson's into his house. They went straight into living room where they were offered a beverage before they sat and conversed about Sarah.

"Sarah...Mr. and Mrs. Wilkerson...come in and sit down. Would you like something cold to drink?"

Donnie answered Paul.

"No thanks, Paul."

Judith followed with her response.

"Like my husband, Donnie…no thanks, Mr. Langston."

Paul thanked the Wilkerson's for bringing his daughter home safely. He expressed much appreciated the gesture.

"Thanks so much for bringing my daughter, Sarah home. I really appreciate you both!"

Judith prepared Paul for what she was about to tell him about Sarah.

"Paul…I guess you've wondering what's been going on with your daughter, Sarah. I've been talking to her more like what a mother would talk about to a daughter; I would call it. Sarah…go ahead!"

"Well…daddy…I want to tell that I love you. I hope what I'm about to tell you, I hope you won't hate me for it! Please…daddy, don't hate me! Daddy…I'm pregnant!"

Sarah finally confessed to her father that she was pregnant, Susan Langston, Sarah's mother walked through the front door while Sarah revealed her pregnancy. Susan became belligerent when she overheard Sarah's confession about her pregnancy to her father.

"You're what! Repeat that, Sarah, I want to make sure I heard you correctly!"

Susan came up closely into Sarah's face in haste while the Wilkerson's and Paul looked on with madness.

"You're what, Sarah, I want to make sure I really heard you correctly!"

Hesitant to tell her mother, Sarah decided to get it over with and tell her mother straight forward about her situation.

"Mama…I'm pregnant!"

"You little whore! What you mean to tell me that you're pregnant! What's wrong with you…you little whore?" Susan questioned Sarah.

Susan, within an instant, hauled off and slapped Sarah very hard in the face. Donnie and Judith watched in horror and disbelief as Susan slapped Sarah violently about the face. Sarah abruptly grabbed her face in disbelief. She was in pain…fearing that her mother would repeat the process. Paul became aggressive towards Susan as he witnessed his daughter being slapped by her mother. Paul hauled off in anger and slaps Susan about the face…repeating the process towards her. Susan fell to the floor immediately after Paul slapped her. Paul expressed his anger in aggression towards Susan.

"You're the whore! Don't you ever in your life touch my daughter again. Some mother you call yourself to our daughter. You're the one out in the street whoring around. Get out of my house! Get up and get out, Susan!"

Paul aggressively grabbed Susan off the floor by her arm and threw her out of the house. Susan stumbled out of the house in disbelief of what Paul had done.

"I'll pack your stuff! I don't want to ever see you around this house, or around Sarah again. I'm fighting you for full custody, Susan, you better believe it!"

Paul slammed the door in Susan's face and locked it. Sarah was holding her face in pain. She became very emotional about her mother hitting her, belittling and hating her for being pregnant.

"I'm so sorry, daddy! I'm so sorry for putting you through this."

"Sarah…you have nothing to be sorry for, I'm a bit saddened about the news though, but what I need to do is support you and the decisions that you and I will be making according to your pregnancy."

Sarah was shocked that her father took the news about her pregnancy so well. Sarah was surprised about how her father took the news about her pregnancy.

"You don't hate me, daddy?" Sarah asked.

"I don't hate you, Sarah! Not in a million years from now." Paul replied. Sarah was crying. She looked right into her father's eyes and she revealed how much her mother hated her for being pregnant.

"I know mama hates me with a passion! Daddy…she came straight out and called me a whore…right here in front of the Wilkerson's. I'm so embarrassed, daddy! I'm no whore, daddy! I've only been with one boy." Paul questioned Sarah about the father of her baby.

"Who is the baby's father, Sarah?"

"A boy named Richard Morris. Daddy...he's a creep and a loser and I'm so stupid! Paul took Sarah into his arms. "You're not stupid, Sarah!" Sarah revealed what Richard been saying about her around the school. "Daddy...Richard has been going around the entire school claiming he's not our baby's father. He is daddy! There's no doubt about it!"

"Richard Morris! Where do he live Sarah?" Paul questioned his daughter. "Maybe we need to pay Richard and his folks a visit. Do you have his address?" Sarah didn't want to reveal Richard's address...frighten of what her life would be like if she revealed her pregnancy to Richard's parents.

"Daddy no! You know what my life will be like if you tell his folks? He'll probably trash me even more around the entire school. I'll be known as the whore of Middleton High, because I got pregnant from that creep. Richard would like nothing more as to destroy my pride and dignity. He's already done that."

Paul threatened to trash Richard, if he trashed his daughter around school.

"Not before I trash him, Sarah!"

Donnie clearly understood Sarah's feelings about what would happen to her if word got out about her pregnancy around school.

"Sarah...that's totally understandable about the way you feel about being trashed and Richard taking responsibility for his actions. These boys now of days need to take charge for their actions and learn to be responsible in life situations like yours." Donnie said.

Paul agreed! "Mr. Wilkerson is right! You know he's right Sarah. I'll handle the part of you getting trashed around school. Don't you worry about that, Sarah."

"Daddy...how are you going to prevent me from being trashed around school? How are you going to prevent that, daddy? You can't be there with me every minute!"

"Don't worry, Sarah about what I'm going to do, I said I'll take care of it."

Judith and Donnie were still very shocked about what happened earlier when Susan hauled off and slapped Sarah in the face. They figured it was uncalled for Susan to do what she did to Sarah, when she needed her the most. Judith and Donnie was in disbelief when Susan turned her back on Sarah and walked away. Judith made her point about what happened earlier at the Langston household. It was very clear about how she felt about Susan.

"Paul...I didn't like the show earlier. Your wife, Susan made me so mad. If you will excuse me, Mr. Langston, because Susan is your wife and Sarah's mother, I just wanted to haul off and slap her myself."

Donnie couldn't believe what Judith intended to do. He also agreed to the fact of the matter that Judith was the better woman in Sarah's case.

"Judith...my God...what's that to say about my wife? But...she's right, Paul. I wanted to haul off and slap Susan too. No offence to you Paul, after what she did to Sarah."

Paul assured the Wilkerson's that there was no problem about the fact of the matter with his wife, Susan. Paul belittled Susan in the presents of the Wilkerson's for her not being a good mother to Sarah. It was the way that he saw her.

"I got to say this Mr. and Mrs. Wilkerson, it's fine. No harm was done to damage Susan's character. Susan gave birth to Sarah; she's less than a mother; she's less than a woman; she's worst; she's no mother! Sarah would have been acting the same way. Thank goodness I'm here for my daughter. Thank you, Mrs. Wilkerson for being an awesome mother figure for Sarah. Thanks for giving her advice on how to be a woman. I wouldn't have belittle Susan if she would have been a good mother to Sarah." Judith responded to Paul with a complement for what she did for his daughter Sarah. "I really appreciate what you said to about being that mother figure for Sarah, that's all I'll ever be to her...a mother figure."

"I got to say, as a woman, I agree with you Paul."

With all the belittling of her mother from her father and the Wilkerson's, Sarah still acknowledged her love for her mother, Susan…no matter what she has done to her in the past. Sarah still loved the woman she called mother, the woman who gave her life beyond her own. Sarah turned towards her dad with tears in her eyes and said, "No matter what, daddy, I still love her as the woman who gave birth to me, but in my heart, Susan is no mother to me… not by a long shot. She will never be where she needs to be and that's in my life, but she will always be in my heart no matter what."

Donnie embraced Sarah.

"Where was Susan when you needed her for that advice is right, Sarah. Now, you're going to experience something and that's giving birth…being a woman before your time…and learning the true meaning of love and being loved. You're going to be a good mother; I just know it Sarah! It's a very important to be."

Chapter Four

"Richard's Indiscretions"

It was late in the afternoon after the long discussion with the Wilkerson's about Sarah's pregnancy. Paul Langston and his daughter, Sarah decided to visit Richard and his parents. Sarah and her father, Paul walked up to the Morris's front door and knocked. Mr. Eddie Morris...Richard's father opened his door and was met by Paul and Sarah Langston.

"Hello...may I help you!" Paul introduced himself and his daughter Sarah to the Morris's.

"Hello sir...I'm here to speak with about your son, Richard."

"And you are?"

"Oh...I'm Paul Langston...and this is my daughter, Sarah Langston. I would like to speak with you about a situation involving your son and my daughter...if you don't mind sir. Can we come in?"

Eddie invited Paul and his daughter, Sarah, into his home.

"Yes...please...come in! Come into the living room."

Paul and Sarah entered into the foyer of the Morris's household. They went straight into the living room and sat down on the couch.

"Thanks sir." Eddie introduced himself to Paul and his daughter Sarah.

"My name is Eddie...Eddie Morris. Nice to meet you. Now.... what is this situation your daughter has with my son?" Paul prepared himself to explain to Richard's father about his and Sarah's visit to his home.

"Well, Mr. Morris!"

"Call me Eddie!"

"Well Eddie...it's of a delicate matter. This has everything to do with my daughter, Sarah and your son, Richard."

Eddie was silenced briefly with concern. He knew that something was not right with the matter of his son Richard and Paul's daughter, Sarah. A surprised Eddie questioned Paul.

"Oh my God.... you're not saying...oh my God...a delicate matter...is your it...is your daughter?"

Paul revealed Sarah's pregnancy to Eddie without hesitation.

"Yes...my daughter, Sarah is pregnant and your son, Richard is the father of her baby", Paul said.

Eddie quickly stood up from the sofa and rushed into the foyer. Paul rushed behind Eddie. He confirmed the news to Eddie. "It's for sure, Eddie." Eddie fiercely paced the foyer of the front door entrance. He was very surprised and shocked by the news of Sarah's pregnancy and the fact that his son, Richard, was the father. "It was no doubt", Paul stated. Eddie still didn't want to believe the fact that Richard was involved in getting Sarah pregnant. He was still in disbelief about Sarah's pregnancy, but he still wanted to know for sure.

"No...no... you got to be kidding! You just got to be kidding, Mr. Langston. How do you really know this?"

Sarah answered the question Eddie had directed mainly towards her father, Paul.

"Because...Mr. Morris, your son Richard was the only boy I've been with, no one else, sir...I promise you that. Richard knows this."

"Hey little lady…are you really sure about this?"

"I'm not lying to you, Mr. Morris about this. I'm serious! Richard is the only one."

Eddie was enraged with anger about the news he received from Paul Langston about his daughter, Sarah. Eddie called out to Richard to come downstairs. He also called for his wife, Charlotte to join in the conversation about their son.

"Okay! Alright! We'll get Richard down here right now, Richard. Little lady…I will assure you, we will get to the bottom of this. Eddie yelled at the bottom of the stairs for Richard in haste. "Richard! Richard! Boy…get your butt down stairs right now boy… right now! Charlotte, you come in here too. You need to hear this!"

Charlotte exited the kitchen with concern about what was going on in the living room with Eddie and his temper.

"What's wrong, Eddie?" Charlotte came into the living room to see what Eddie was upset about.

"Charlotte…you'll find out when our son reaches the end of his path down at the bottom of these stairs."

Richard finally came downstairs. He turned towards the living room and saw Sarah and her father, Paul. Sarah and her father, Paul was staring at the stairway as Richard came down. Richard was very insecure about seeing Sarah and her father, Paul sitting in the living room. Richard gave a hard and stoned look. He decided to play it off and acted like he didn't know what was going on.

"What's up pops? Whoa…. what's going on here? Sarah…what are you doing here?"

Knowingly…Richard tried to play like he didn't know a thing. Sarah stood up and walked over to Richard. She faced him directly with her answer.

"Richard…I think you know why I'm here, quit trying to play me on this one."

Richard angrily stared at Sarah like she was a piece of meat with extreme haste. Richard's parents continued questioning him about Sarah's pregnancy.

"Oh no, Sarah, you're not going to put this on me."

Eddie questioned Richard directly as Charlotte looked on. Richard looked over at his father, Eddie. He was reluctant for a moment before he came clean about Sarah's pregnancy and his involvement.

"Oh yes, Richard...oh yes! You that child's daddy? Don't lie to your daddy. Don't lie to my face boy?"

Charlotte turned and looked over at Richard.

"Eddie...what's going on? Richard...did what, Eddie? Richard, what did you do?"

Richard was reluctant to answer his mother's question.

"I don't know what's going on mama. I think I'm being framed! Richard looked back at his father Eddie. "Well...sort of daddy."

Eddie got beyond frustrated with Richard.

"What do you mean sort of...boy? There is no such thing as sort of!"

"Pops...I don't know!" Richard looked at Sarah once again like stone.

Charlotte cried out in shock.

"Richard...you got a baby on the way?"

"Okay, mama...yeah...yeah...yeah!"

Charlotte became emotional about the fact that Richard got Sarah pregnant.

"What's wrong with you, boy? After all, we talk about you do this to me and your father. How could you, Richard!" Richard tried to explain himself to his mother, Charlotte.

"Mama...you don't understand!", Richard yelled out to his mother.

Eddie gave Richard an ultimatum.

"You're going to get out of this house tomorrow and you're going find you a job Richard. You're not going to be lolly gagging and lagging around here in this house. You're going take care of your responsibility you got in that girl stomach, instead of running around in this house acting like you're a mac daddy wannbe pimp."

Paul tried to assure his daughter, Sarah of a promise he made to her just before they arrived at the Morris's household to speak with

Richard's parents…so that she wouldn't be verbally trashed around Middleton High by their son, Richard.

"I just want to say, Mr. Morris. Eddie! I want to be sure of this; I made my daughter, Sarah a promise that she wouldn't be trashed around the school. I want to assure that Sarah's reputation will not be trashed verbally or tarnished around the entire school by your son, Richard."

Eddie responded. He assured Paul that his daughter, Sarah will not be trashed around the entire school by his son.

"I will make Richard keeps his mouth shut, I will be sure of that, Mr. Langston. Richard will keep a civil tongue in his mouth, or I'll pull it out and he won't be able to utter a word to anyone."

Sarah was relieved with the responses given by her father and Richard's father, Eddie, that her reputation would not be tarnished or trashed verbally in any way. Sarah looked up to her father and smiled.

"Thanks daddy." She then turned to Mr. and Mrs. Morris. She greeted them with thanks.

"Thanks Mr. and Mrs. Morris." The Morris's responded back to Sarah.

"No problem little lady. I will make sure that my son doesn't run his big mouth at the school house…..you'll be sure that will not happen."

Charlotte apologized to Sarah.

"I'm so sorry about this, Sarah and Mr. Langston and about our son's short comings." Paul assured Charlotte that it was no need to apologize for their son, Richard short comings.

"No need, Mrs. Morris. No need! All of us need to come together as decent human beings and come to a solution about what has happened and how we all can cope with this situation between our two children."

Eddie agreed with Paul concerning their families coming together to cope with Sarah's pregnancy and for Richard to take responsibility for his actions concerning Sarah and her pregnancy.

"I agree with you, Paul. I totally agree! We need to come together on this very delicate matter sure enough."

"Well Eddie…Charlotte…my daughter and I are going home. It was nice to meet you, Eddie. Paul shook Eddie's hand as he was getting ready to exit the Morris household. "Mrs. Morris."

"Charlotte…It was nice to meet you as well."

Eddie glanced over at Richard like he was Medusa. Eddie's look towards Richard was a look for turning Richard into stone. Eddie then look back at Paul and Sarah with a smile.

"Since we're going to be grandparents, we look forward to seeing you and your daughter again. Paul responded.

"I'm glad we came and talked about this. Thanks for having me and my daughter over on such notice."

Paul and his daughter, Sarah exited the Morris household. They walked down the walk way to their car. Richard looked out the window of the living room in extreme and total anger towards Sarah. Eddie closed the front door and confronted Richard into his face.

"What a situation! What has come over you, boy? You think this is funny? You think this situation you help create is some kind of play toy? This is very serious, Richard! I'm going to make sure you're going to take care of this matter, boy, you can believe that!" Eddie walked away from Richard.

Richard looked over at his mother, Charlotte. He proceeded to walked away from his mother. Charlotte looked at Richard with disappointment. She stopped Richard in his tracks and gave him an ultimatum.

"How could you, Richard, after all we talked about?"

"I'm sorry…I'm sorry…mama!" Richard almost silently said. Charlotte responded back to Richard.

"I'm also going to make sure, as well as your father, that you don't verbally trash Sarah around that entire school, either. If I hear anything about it from anyone around that school…or in the neighborhood, …if I hear a whisper…or a peep…or so much as a he say-she say rumor, I'm going to beat the ever loving crap out of you; I promise, and I'll make sure your friends watch too."

Charlotte walked away abruptly from Richard. She left him alone, standing in the middle of the living room floor in thought of what he helped cause and for not accepting the fact like a man that he was in fact going to be a father.

Meanwhile at the Wilkerson household, Emily made a telephone call to Sarah. It was about the situation her pregnancy. Sarah answered Emily's call. Emily was the first to reply to Sarah

"How are you, Sarah? How is it going with you? And how did it go with Richard's parents, the Morris's today and with Richard?"

Sarah responded to Emily.

"I'm doing much better, Emily. Richard confesses to being the father of my baby right in front of his parents. There was no way for him to deny it."

"You're kidding, Sarah! How did Richard's parents get him to confess about the baby?"

Emily questioned Sarah about Richard's confession.

"Well, Emily, …his dad was the aggressive one…kind of hard notch…and he was aggravated with Richard. He was mainly the one who that got Richard to confess about my pregnancy. Mr. Morris looked as if he wanted to kill Richard when he came downstairs and confronted my father and I and his mother too."

Emily was shocked at the way Sarah described Richard's father Eddie when was told about her pregnancy and Richard's involvement.

"Oh my God, Sarah, you're kidding! What was his mother like?"

Emily was anxious to know what Richard's mother was like according to Richard's father Eddie.

"Emily…Mrs. Morris had a little spice in her voice as well. She had the look like she wanted to slap Richard silly if you ask me." Emily decided to call her friend Denise in a threeway call.

"Sarah…do you mind if I call Denise and let her in on this? She would love to hear this about you and Richard?" Sarah gave Emily permission to include their friend Denise in their conversations.

"Oh, of course, Emily. I don't mind if you let Denise in on our conversation."

Emily placed Sarah on hold while she made a three-way the call to their classmate and friend, Denise Collins. She waited until the call came through to include her in hers and Sarah's conversations. Denise spoke from the receiving end of her telephone at home.

"Hello…is this you, Emily?"

Denise on the receiving end.

"Yes…this is Emily, Denise. What are you doing right now?" Emily asked.

"Nothing, Emily. I'm fine." Denise replied to Emily.

"Denise…can you hold please while I get Sarah back on the phone?"

"Okay…I'll be here, Emily." Denise was put on hold until she got Sarah back on the phone.

Emily received Sarah back on line. Sarah responded on the receiving end.

"Emily…you're there?" Sarah asked.

"I'm here, Sarah! Go ahead, Denise. Sarah's on the line."

"Hello Sarah. How are you doing?" Denise asked.

"I'm doing great. I'm dealing with my pregnancy very well and what happened at the Morris's house today. Promise me, Denise you won't say anything to anyone at school or anywhere else about what I'm going to tell you. Promised me!"

"I promise, Sarah!" Denise promised Sarah that she want spill the beans about her pregnancy at school.

"My daddy was wonderful today. We went to the Morris's and we talked with Richard's parents about not verbally trashing me around the entire school about my pregnancy. Believe me, Denise, Richard's parents were hard notch about the whole situation with me and with Richard. They looked like they wanted to kill Richard right then and there."

"Okay, I understand that perfectly, Sarah!" Denise said.

"So what we're talking about is keeping this secret about what was said to the Morris's and your pregnancy and Richard being the father of your baby between just us at all times without any interference from anyone else?"

"That's right, Denise. I can tell you…Richard looked like death in his eyes. He thought he would die after his parents got through with him." Sarah responded.

"I can't believe it, Sarah, what you're telling me about him and his parents. He really deserves what he gets. He's a creep and a bad dream…a dirt bag!"

Emily re-joined the conversation with Sarah and Denise.

"I hear you, Denise. Richard has been doing other people wrong forever and a day."

It was getting late and Sarah had to call it a night with Emily and Denise. Emily! Denise! Well girls…I can't really talk too long tonight. I got to turn in and get some sleep for school tomorrow. I'll see you in the courtyard tomorrow."

The girls all hung up at the same time. Judith in the background. She informed Emily that it was time for bed, so that she would be ready for school, bright and early the next day.

"Emily…you need to be in bed. You got school tomorrow. No more phone tonight."

"Okay, mama! Good night mama." Emily said while preparing herself for bed.

"Good night, Emily." Judith shouted from her bedroom.

Daniel was in the background. He proceeded to insult his sister before turning in for bed.

"Good night…crater face!"

Emily returned the insults back to her brother, Daniel.

"Can it! Dirt bag!"

Judith was in the background. She demolished the insults between Emily and Daniel.

"Come on you two. I want you to stop all that foolishness and name calling. I've already told both of you about this. Now…go to sleep down there!"

Emily turned off the light and immediately went off to sleep."

Chapter Five

"Richard's Revenge on Sarah"

The next morning at Middleton High, Sarah was at her locker. She retrieved some books she needed for her first class. Richard approached Sarah from behind. He pressed up close behind her. He was very angry with Sarah. Richard shouted into Sarah's ear in haste. He was very angry with Sarah for embarrassing him in front of his parents about her about her pregnancy. Emily and Denise stood off from a distance as they watched and overheard Richard threatening Sarah about what had occurred at his house.

"You think that you can embarrass me in front of my parents like that, Sarah?"

Richard grabbed Sarah by the arms as he leaned over her shoulder into her face.

"You…made me look stupid; I was looking like I was a heel; you made me feel like an idiot right in front of my parents." Richard threaten Sarah with haste. "Do you know I could kill you right now!"

Sarah feared for her safety and her life at that particular moment. She looked away from Richard as she trembled with fear. Sarah responded to Richard's threats against her.

"Richard...I wasn't trying to make you look stupid, or like a heel, or an idiot in front of your parents. I was only trying to make you take responsibility of this situation we both created. We got a baby growing inside of me. All I wanted for you to do is take responsibility for the baby. I'm sorry, but...you're taking it the wrong way." Richard stared at Sarah with a look that will kill a tick.

"Yeah...I bet you're sorry! You embarrassing me in front of my parents."

Richard pressed up against Sarah again. He leaned over her shoulder into her face again. He threatened Sarah.

"Sarah...no one, and I mean no one embarrasses me...ever. You hear me, Sarah! No one gets away with that with me. Who do you think you are, Sarah! I'm going to let you know this for sure. Your mine! Understand that fully! All of you! Your mine! Always watch your back, Sarah...in all directions!"

Sarah was shaken with fear. She was very afraid for her safety and her life. She responded to Richard's threats once again.

"Are you threatening me, Richard!"

"I'm not threatening you Sarah. I'm telling you! Don't forget who you're dealing with baby. I will hurt you. Remember that!" Richard walked off while looking back at Sarah in haste.

Emily and Denise ran up to a frightened and shaken Sarah. They gave her "guarded" moral support after they heard Richard threatening her. Denise was the most concerned about Sarah.

"We heard Richard threaten you, Sarah. Are you're okay?" Denise questioned Sarah...fearing for her friend's life. Sarah assured Denise that she was fine after receiving Richard's threats towards her.

"Don't worry about me, Denise. I'm fine! No problem! He's just being Mr. Big Shot."

A very worried Emily gave Sarah some words of advice about Richard and the threat he made towards her.

"Sarah…I don't think so! He didn't look or sound like he was sympathetic to you, or the baby and the situation you're in with him. He looked and sounded like he wanted to hurt you, Sarah. Richard want to hurt you really bad." Emily tried to warn Sarah about Richard anger and the threats he made against her.

Denise agreed with Emily's advice to Sarah about Richard's threats towards her.

"I agree with Emily! You can't play around with someone like Richard Sarah. He's evil! The way he was looking at you gave me bad chills throughout my body. He's a total scum bag, Sarah. You don't play around with guys like that; I'm serious about this, Sarah."

"Everything is going to be fine, Emily…Denise. You'll see! Stop staring at me! He can't do anything to me with everyone standing around. His parents promised me nothing will happen to me. Richard is just blowing off steam. He'll get over it! We've been through this before. Richard has never hit me before when we were going together."

Worried and scared for Sarah, Emily decided to walk home with Sarah after school as a precaution and for her safety. Emily feared that Richard could be anywhere and he would harm Sarah.

"Maybe one of us, or both of us should walk home with you today, Sarah. – just in case Richard tries something. I'm scared and worried about you, Sarah."

"You're taking this way out of proportion, Emily…Denise…the both of you. I know you both mean well. I'll be alright. Please… Emily and Denise…don't worry about this. I'll be fine! You'll see."

Sarah turned and walked away from Emily and Denise. Denise called out to Sarah…fearing the inevitable. Denise ran part of the ways behind Sarah. She called out to Sarah again.

"Sarah…. Sarah…. wait a minute…. Sarah!"

Sarah looked back for a brief moment to look at her friends Emily and Denise. She turned around and continued to walk home. Sarah in fact…refused to listen to the inevitable about Richard from her friends, Emily and Denise. Concerned for Sarah's well-being and safety, Emily conversed with Denise in the school courtyard about Sarah shutting them out from protecting her from Richard.

"What are we going to do about Sarah, Denise? She's not listening to either one of us about Richard. We all talked about this over the phone last night. Why is she doing this?" Disappointed with

attitude about Richard and turning a deaf ear to the situation with Richard. Denise tried to determine what changed Sarah's mind about Richard's demands and threats against her by Richard.

"I don't know, Emily. Something must have happened when Sarah got off the phone last night. Maybe...something must have happened to her on way to school. I don't know, Emily."

Denise tried to determine the fate of Sarah's decision making when it comes to Richard and his threats against Sarah. Emily gave Denise an ultimatum to wait for in the courtyard after school.

"We need to wait for Sarah in the courtyard after school, Denise. I don't trust Richard lurking around this school and this courtyard for a second. We both need to be here for Sarah at the end of the day for Sarah, even if she doesn't listen to reason with us. We owe Sarah that as our friend!"

"Alright Emily, let's do it! Meet me right here in the courtyard today after school. Sarah will be here too; I know she will."

Emily and Denise went their separate ways until school ended.

It was the afternoon. School day ended with the last bell ringing. The entire student body filled the courtyard behind the school. Emily and Denise met out on the courtyard as planned. They waited patiently for Sarah to show, so that they can walk home together. Emily looked around for Sarah in the crowds of students and teachers.

"We'll stand here, Denise, and wait for Sarah to show up so we can all walk home together. I really hope Sarah show up." Denise looked around the courtyard for Sarah. She didn't like the feel, or the atmosphere. It felt like something bad was about to happen.

"Emily...I really don't like the atmosphere around here, not one bit. I fear Richard is haunting this entire courtyard. I think about the way he threatened Sarah this morning. He really scares me to the quick."

"I know what you mean, Denise, I feel it too!"

Emily was worried. She looked around fiercely for Sarah. Emily called out for Sarah several times. Emily saw Sarah from a distance in the crowd of students and teachers. She called out to Sarah once again. Emily waved from a distance for Sarah to come over to where she and Denise was located in the courtyard."

"Sarah...please...over here! Over here!"

Denise called out to Sarah again.

"Sarah! Over here!"

Sarah saw Emily and Denise waving for her to come over to them. She emerged out of the crowds of students and teachers. Sarah was still shaken with fear from Richard's threats against her earlier that morning at her locker. She didn't show any fear, or was she shaken in front of her friends about what happened earlier that morning at her locker with Richard. She refused to not let what happened bother her any further that day.

"Hey Emily...Denise...are you both still worried about what happened this morning with Richard?"

Worried and confused, Emily conversed with Sarah about her actions about Richard and his threats against her.

"Sarah...Denise and I are trying to help you. I didn't like the way Richard was looking at you this morning when he threatened you, and the way he threatened you. Richard really scares me, Sarah." Emily continued to turn a deaf ear to her friend demand and Richard threats against her.

"Come on, Emily! We've been through this before this morning. Richard...he wouldn't hurt me like that. He's harmless! We talked about this briefly last night on the phone. He's harmless! He acted like a wimp in front of his parents."

Denise revealed to Emily and Sarah about her thoughts after they talked on the phone.

"Well Sarah. Emily. Last night was different in a whole lot of ways. I thought about it, Sarah. I thought about you! After we all got off the phone last night and what we talked about what happened at the Morris's house and then this morning, then Richard threatens you." Sarah looked at Denise with a straight and worried look on her face.

"Okay Denise...I'll take this situation into consideration, I promise you. I'm going to walk home. Nothing bad is going to happen to me. His dad and my daddy promised that he will not do me or the baby any harm, or trash me verbally around here at school or anywhere else."

Emily suggested to Sarah about walking home with her.

"Sarah...us walk home with you." Sarah turned to Emily and assured that she will be fine walking home from the courtyard.

"Emily...I'm fine! I think I can walk home without getting hurt. I'll see you both later on and I love you both. I'll call you!"

Alone and shaken...Sarah was really frightened by the possibilities that Richard could be anywhere. She ultimately decided to walk home alone instead. Emily and Denise continued to worry about Sarah as they watched her walk home alone from the courtyard. Emily gave Sarah her last warning about Richard.

"Sarah...please be careful! Look around you at all times. If you see Richard...scream out as loud as you possible could. Please... be careful and take care of yourself. Please call us when you arrive home."

Sarah looked back at Emily and Denise and made a promise that she would contact them when she arrived home.

"I promise, Emily. I promise!"

Sarah walked farther and farther away from the school courtyard. Emily and Denise could not see her anymore. They were still very concerned for Sarah and her safety and well-being, even if they didn't follow their own advice and walked home with her.

Ten minutes into her walk, Sarah became very shaken and unaware of her surroundings. She was consumed with fear. She tried not to visualize the possible whereabouts of Richard and where he might turn up, while she walked home alone. Sarah tried not to think of Richard, or his threats against her earlier. And then...all of a sudden and without doubt, Sarah was spotted by Richard and his friends Kevin Osborne and Luther Rollins. Richard was very belligerent when he yelled out to Sarah.

"Sarah...you mine Sarah!"

Richard fiercely rushed up to Sarah. He confronted her with the intentions of harming her. Sarah was completely stopped in her tracks. She feared the inevitable, as she feared for her life... knowingly she would in fact be harmed by her Richard. Sarah slowly walked around Richard. She walked quickly and didn't look back. Richard stopped Sarah in her track once again. Sarah looked into Richard eyes. She was very silent and still she was consumed with fear. Sarah finally asked Richard about his intentions about harming her.

"Richard...what do you want with me? I'm sorry for what happened at your parent's house. I'm sorry if I embarrassed you in front of them, but it is what it is." Richard stared at Sarah like Medusa. It was a very scary stare...like he wanted to turn Sarah and their unborn baby into stone.

"I want you, Sarah! I want all of you!"

Richard started attacking Sarah...beating her about the face. She tried to run away. Richard caught up with Sarah. She tried once again tried defend herself and her unborn baby she was carrying from the extremely hard blows that Richard was inflicting upon her face and body in a violent rage. Richard was filled with rage for Sarah ever since she and her father Paul came to his house to reveal to his parents, Eddie and Charlotte about her pregnancy. Richard continued to take his rage out on Sarah from the embarrassment that he sustained from revealing her pregnancy to Richard's parents. Emily kept fighting and trying to defend herself and her unborn baby from all of Richard's blows that was continuously inflicted on her. Sarah yelled out to Richard frantically, fearing for her life and her unborn baby.

"Stop it, Richard! What are you doing?" Sarah screamed out very loud. No one heard Sarah screaming for her life.

"You're hurting me, Richard! The baby! The baby, Richard! Stop it!"

Sarah yelled frantically for someone to come and to help her. Richard's friends Kevin and Luther cowardly ran away, leaving Sarah to fend for herself against Richard.

"Someone, help me! Please…someone…help me!"

Richard continued fiercely pounding on Sarah like she was a punching bag, with no remorse for her, or their baby. Sarah was on the ground. She was in a lot of pain from the blows and punches in the face and body she sustained from Richard.

Ten minutes after Sarah left the courtyard of the school, Emily and Denise felt guilty for not walking home with Sarah. They left the school courtyard to catch up to Sarah on her way home.

"I don't know, Denise. Maybe we should have gone with Sarah, no matter what she said, or even if she didn't think or believe she was in danger from that creep Richard. Emily responded as she looked around for Sarah. Denise acknowledged to Emily about Richard's evil ways.

"I've always known that something was not right with Richard from the start. What a creep! I swear, Emily!" Denise replied.

"Denise, I just can't understand why Sarah was acting like nothing we said over the phone or here at school mattered." Emily said while looking around for Sarah.

"I guess Sarah has turned a blind eye to the fact that Richard was dangerous. Of course, he's going to act like a wimp in front of his parents as Sarah states, but…when Richard is alone…."

Emily quickly interrupted Denise

"He's going to act out his anger and aggression for Sarah, because embarrassed him in front of his parents. He said that she made him look like an idiot…and a heel. Denise…I truly believe he will get revenge on Sarah…if he hasn't already!"

"Oh Emily…let's hurry and catch up to Sarah. It's only been a short time since she left the courtyard. We need to get to her before Richard does."

"I hear you, Denise. But…I already think it's too late. Ten minutes is a very short time, but that's too long for me to even think that Sarah is okay, because Richard could be anywhere. Emily and Denise started looking for Sarah again. Let's go Denise!"

Emily and Denise rushed from the courtyard to catch up with Sarah. They called out to Sarah. Emily and Denise looked around. They saw no trace of their friend Sarah anywhere in sight. Emily panicked.

"I don't see Sarah anywhere, Denise. This is the route she takes every single day when she walks home from school from the courtyard."

Denise panicked. Emily and Denise began their search for their friend Sarah. They looked around every corner for at least three blocks. Still…there was no trace of Sarah.

Both Emily and Denise continued to call out for Sarah. She was no were to be found. Not a single trace of Sarah. Emily looked in the bushes and everywhere she could thing think of looking. Denise and Emily went to the first house they came in contact with. Denise walked towards the house where she saw an old woman sitting inside her home watching television. She knocked at the old woman's door in order to get her attention. The old woman got up to open her front door to a panicked Denise.

"Hello…hello! I need your help…if you don't mind. I really need your help! I need you to call the police, please…Madame."

"Little lady…what's going on?"

Emily was panicking. Emily answered the old woman about the disappearance of their Sarah. Emily questioned the old woman about her friend Sarah.

"My friend and I are wondering if you've seen a pregnant girl walk by your house earlier. We think she may be in trouble. She has a very violent boyfriend who want to hurt her. Our friend is missing! We need you to call the police…please!"

The old woman did not hesitate. She picked up the telephone and she immediately called the police after she was informed by Emily and Denise about Sarah's disappearance.

"Okay, little ladies, I called 9-1-1 for the police."

Denise proceeded to look around for Sarah.

"Oh my God, where could Sarah be?" Emily fiercely looked around for Sarah. Still...no trace of her.

"I don't think she couldn't have gotten this far, especially in her condition."

"We should have walked home with Sarah Emily. Denise blamed herself.

"What kind of friends are we to Sarah to let her walk home alone, knowing that Richard had threaten to hurt her earlier during the day. I think we both need to share the blame for this one." Emily agreed with Denise about sharing the blame for Sarah's disappearance.

"There are no other way of putting this, Denise, we should of have walked home with Sarah." Denise started back tracking for Sarah's path.

"Emily...I think I'm going to back track; I'm going to look for Sarah a little farther down until the police arrives." Emily agreed.

"I'll stay here until Sarah...if she turns up, or the police arrive. Please let me know if you find something Denise...okay."

"Okay Emily!"

Denise started her own search party for Sarah before the police arrived. Meanwhile...at the old woman's house, the old woman questioned Emily about Sarah in order to determine the route she take every day.

The old lady asked Emily questions about her friend Sarah.

"Your friend...what did you say her name is? Does she take this route on way home every single day?"

"Her name is Sarah. And yes ma'am! She takes this route every single day. She lives just a few blocks from your house." Emily replied to the old woman.

"I usually sit at the window. I watch my television and sometimes, then I take a brief glance out of my window and I usually see a young lady pass by my house. She looks to be your age. She walks pass my house every single day. She would also wave at when she passes by. Today of all days, I didn't see her walk pass my house today. Maybe that could be your friend we're talking about?" Emily took the old woman words into consideration. She had a thought about Sarah's whereabouts.

"Oh my Lord...my friend Denise is out right now back tracking looking for our friend, Sarah. She might be hurt and we maybe have passed along the way and didn't see her. Oh my God!"

Denise was looking around in the bushes for anything that didn't belong there. Just blocks from the old woman's house, Denise saw some school books under a bush. She decided to look around into the bushes mysteriously. They were in fact Sarah's school books. Denise panicked! She was very upset and afraid what she might discover, besides Sarah's school books. Denise ran back to the old woman's house. She yelled out for Emily to come and take a look at what she found in the bushes a blocks from the old woman's house. Emily ran to the location where Denise found Sarah's school books under the bushes. Emily questioned Denise about Sarah's school books and no trace of Sarah.

"Oh my God...did you find Sarah? Did you see anything else, Denise?" Denise replied to Emily.

"No, Emily! Denise was in tears. I didn't see anything else. I saw only Sarah's books in the bushes, but I didn't see Sarah. Oh my God! Where's Sarah?" Both Emily and Denise embraced each other. They worried they would never find Sarah hurt, or alive.

The police arrived almost immediately after the old woman called emergency 911. The first officer on location was Officer Donleavy. He pursued the case for missing Sarah Langston. Officer Donleavy introduced himself to Emily and Denise and the old woman.

"Hello...I'm Officer Donleavy. Someone called and reported a missing person?" The officer questioned the Emily, Denise and the old woman. The old woman answered the officers question.

"I did, Officer. I made the call. These ladies' said their friend is missing." The old woman pointed out Emily and Denise to the officer Donleavy about their missing friend, Sarah. The officer questioned Emily first about Sarah.

"What happened here? Officer Donleavy questioned Emily.

"The old woman said that your friend is missing. What's her name?" Emily answered the officer's question identifying her friend Sarah to the officer.

"Her name is Sarah Langston officer. She was walking home from the school courtyard. She left about ten minutes before my friend and left the school courtyard."

Denise disclosed to Officer Donleavy about the threats Richard made to Sarah earlier during the just before school started.

"Sarah had an incident this morning with her boyfriend, Richard Morris. He verbally threatened her with intentions of harming her in the worst way possible. He really wanted to hurt our friend officer. He made me shake like I was in fear for my life."

"Who is this boyfriend?" Officer Donleavy questioned Denise.

"His name is Richard Morris." Denise replied to the officer.

Emily interrupted the officers line of questioning with her friend, Denise.

"Officer Donleavy, Sarah's boyfriend, Richard said that she embarrassed and made him look like an idiot in front of his parents. Our friend, Sarah is pregnant! She told his parents about her pregnancy yesterday at his parents house. This morning...he felt threatened by what she said to his parents and decided that he would pay her back by beating the ever loving tar of her just for embarrassing him in front of his parents about her pregnancy. That is what this is about!"

Denise added more commentary to Richard's verbal threats he made to Sarah during the morning before classes administered.

"He said no one threatens him and that's at any time. No one! Richard also said that our friend, Sarah that she belonged to him. It was like no one else can have you, or is going to have you ever. It was the way he said it, very cold and evil. Something like that!"

Denise remembered seeing Sarah's school books in the bushes. She informed Officer Donleavy of her mysterious findings.

"Oh...I forgot! Officer Donleavy...I went out to look for Sarah. One or two blocks back, I found some of her school books in the bushes, but no sight of Sarah. I decided not to touch anything. I didn't want to include my finger prints on evidence, but I had to look to see if in fact those were my friends school books. Denise started to panic again about what she had done. "Officer...I had to look in the books to see if they are in fact hers." Denise said to the officer.

"You shouldn't have touched those books. Did you walk anywhere else around that scene?" The officer replied to Denise as he touched base the importance...if in fact...of a crime scene.

"No sir...I didn't! I'll show you where I found Sarah's books." Officer Donleavy informed the girls once again about the importance of a crime scene before leaving to investigate its location.

"Okay, little lady, let's take a ride to the scene. Be careful when we arrive there, I don't want you girls near anything, or around the scene...even the bushes. Understand me ladies, there could be foot print's, DNA, and other materials scattered all around the location where the books were found. I don't want them disturbed... understand me? Let's go!"

Officer Donleavy and the girls arrived at the scene where Denise found Sarah's school books. The officer exited his police cruiser to take a look around the scene where Sarah's school books were spotted in the bushes. Officer Donleavy discovered Sarah two yards over from where her school books were located. Sarah was lying partially under a large bush. Officer Dunleavy was startled about his discovery of Sarah.

"Sweet Holy Jesus! It's your friend, Sarah."

Emily was totally shocked at what she saw. She began to run where Sarah was spotted. Officer Donleavy grabbed Emily by the arms. He stopped her from running towards the bush where Sarah was located in order to keep the crime scene from being disturbed.

"Sarah! Sarah! Is she dead?" Emily shouted out in fear that Sarah may be dead.

"No…no…don't go over there. I got to close this area off. I got to call for backup. Do not go pass this area, Miss. I'm going to check to see if if your friend is still alive. Stay here!"

Officer Donleavy taped the area with the police caution tape to prevent anyone from crossing over and contaminating of the crime scene. Officer Donleavy walked over to Sarah. He saw that she was brutally beaten about the face and almost her entire body. Officer Donleavy became emotionally disturbed by Sarah's appearance. He remained alert…holding back his emotions, after what he had seen. It was his job to do so under any circumstances. Sarah's appearance nearly took toll on Officer Dunleavy and his way of thinking. Denise and Emily were already emotional after seeing Sarah and the condition she was in. They feared for the worst for Sarah. Emily demanded answers from the officer about Sarah's condition.

"Officer Donleavy…is Sarah alive? Please tell me if she okay?"

Officer Donleavy leaned over and checked Sarah for a pulse.

"She seems fine alright. Her pulse very is strong and that's a good thing. We want know anything else until she is stabilized and ready to be transported to the hospital. She is alive! I'm going to radio in for a paramedic. I would like you ladies to please be out of the way when the paramedic arrive to the crime scene. "They will need the room to get to the crime scene."

The paramedics arrived within minutes to the crime scene to transport Sarah to the local hospital for treatment. The paramedics carefully placed Sarah on the stretcher and into the ambulance. Shocked with disbelief…Emily noticed the brutality of Sarah's face and body. She was filled with black and blue bruises, a busted lip and two black eyes. Emily cried out to Sarah in disbelief.

"Oh my Lord, Sarah…what did Richard do to you? My God Sarah!"

Slightly conscious…Sarah muffled under her voice in total and in extreme agony from her brutal beating at the hands of Richard.

"It was Richard! It was Richard!" Sarah looked over at her friends Emily and Denise. She apologized to both girls for not letting them walk and follow her home from the school courtyard.

Officer Donleavy abruptly questioned Sarah without hesitation in order to get a statement about the brutality of her beating involving Richard. Officer Donleavy filed a report before Sarah was sedated and transported to the hospital.

"Sarah…can you answer some more questions? This would only take a brief moment of your time, then I'll let the paramedics transport you immediately to the local hospital. I just need some information concerning your brutal beating involving your boyfriend, Richard Morris."

Sarah struggled in extreme agony from the bruises that were inflicted on her face and body in order to answer Officer Donleavy's questions to the best of her knowledge. Sarah continued to struggle as she muffled under her voice to answer Officer Dunleavy's questions.

"Yes Officer. I will answer. I want you to get Richard! He hurt me! He hurt me very bad! He hurt me!"

"Sarah…what I need to know from you before I let the paramedics transport you to the hospital; I need to know where this Richard Morris live? Can you tell me his address…so I can go and pick him up?" Sarah muffled. "5-7-4 Oak Leaf!"

"Okay Sarah. I'm going to let the paramedic transport you to the hospital now. I will be picking up this Richard Morris at the address you've given me. Thanks for your cooperation. Be well, Sarah!"

Denise climbed into the ambulance with Sarah. She was immediately transported to the local hospital.

"I'm riding with Sarah to the hospital, what are you going to do, Emily?" Denise asked Emily.

"I'm going home so I can let my parents know what happened to Sarah. I'll call Mr. Langston to inform him about what happened to Sarah." Emily stared at her friend Sarah in the ambulance in disbelief, she was so beaten up.

"Okay Emily! I'll call you form from the hospital Denise."

The paramedics transported Sarah with Denise in tow to the local hospital. Officer Donleavy decided to transport Emily home as a precaution just in case Richard was still on the run. Emily was most appreciative to Officer Donleavy for transporting her home.

"Thanks officer for the lift." Officer Donleavy thanked Emily.

"I'll get you home safely."

Officer Donleavy proceeded to transport Emily home safely. After dropping off Emily at home, Officer Donleavy arrived to the Morris's household to question and possibly arrest Richard. The officer exited his cruiser. He then proceeded to the front door of the Morris's household. He knocked. Eddie Morris answered the door, unaware of his son, Richard's fate.

"Hello officer…is there something wrong, sir? May I help you?" Officer Donleavy informed Eddie that he was looking for his son Richard.

"Hello sir…I'm Officer Donleavy. I'm looking for a Richard Morris. Does he live here?" Eddie replied.

"He's my son, Officer Donleavy. He lives here. What is it he's done?" Officer Donleavy responded to Eddie's questions.

"I just need to ask your son a few questions about an incident that happened recently."

Charlotte Morris peeped out of the kitchen. She noticed the police officer questioning Eddie about their son, Richard.

"Eddie…why is the police at our door? What is going on, Eddie with Richard with that we need to know about?"

"The officer here wants to ask our son some questions about an incident involving him that happened recently."

"Questions! What kind of questions?"

Officer Donleavy informed the Morris's about their son's indiscretions involving Sarah Langston and what happened to her as she walked home from the school courtyard.

"I have reason to believe that your son, Richard was involved in an brutal assault and battery of a young woman earlier today as walked she walked home from the school courtyard today. According to the young woman's friends, the victim was identified as Sarah Langston. I just want to ask your son a few questions about

Miss. Langston and his involvement in her brutal beating. She was beaten so brutally; she was not recognizable."

Shocked and frustrated! Eddie belligerently called for Richard to come downstairs when he learned from Officer Donleavy about Sarah's condition.

"Sarah Langston. That's Richard's girlfriend. I'll call him down stairs right now. It will take just a moment, Officer Donleavy. Eddie continued to call for Richard.

"Richard…get your butt down here right now, boy! Right now!"

Richard came downstairs. He acted like as though he was clueless.

"What's going on, pop? What you call me down here for, pop? What is that officer doing here?"

Eddie catches onto Richard and his clueless acts.

"Don't you get smart with me, boy. You know darn well what's going on! I'll knock you into the middle of the third week. The officer wants to ask you some questions about a brutal assault that occurred earlier today on your way home today. You better not lie either, boy!"

Officer Donleavy assured Eddie that his son, Richard, wasn't going to be charged for the crime against at that point. He questioned Richard about the brutal assault on Sarah Langston.

"Your son hasn't been charged yet, Mr. Morris."

"Call me Eddie." Officer Donleavy continued to ask Eddie's permission to ask Richard questions about Sarah's brutal assault.

"Eddie…Mr. Morris, I would like to ask your son some questions about his girlfriend, Sarah Langston."

"Okay, Officer Donleavy, you have my permission."

Richard continued to act as though he was still clueless about the facts and the problem he caused in Sarah's brutal beating. Richard asked about Sarah whereabouts.

"Sarah Langston! What happened to my girlfriend Sarah?"

Officer Donleavy immediately refreshed Richard memory about his involvement and the extent of the problem in which he caused in the brutal beating of his girlfriend, Sarah.

"She was brutally assaulted earlier today, after leaving school courtyard on her way home. She was found later afterwards under a brush just a few blocks from her home. She was severely and brutally beaten about the face, disfiguring it completely." Richard continued to deny he had any involvement with Sarah's brutal beating. Officer Donleavy continue to grill Richard about Sarah's brutal beating. "You're telling me you don't know what happened to your girlfriend Richard?"

Richard was nervous about being found out what he did to Sarah. Right before the Officer Donleavy, Richard lifted his right hand to rub the side of his face. Officer Donleavy immediately noticed a fresh injury on Richard's right hand.

"No Officer...I don't know anything about a brutal assault on anyone." Officer Donleavy quickly grabbed Richard by his right hand.

"What happened to your hand?"

Richard snatch his hand from the officer and placed it on his side.

"Ah...so you're telling me that's nothing!"

Richard weaved his web of deceit to Officer Donleavy about what happened to his right hand. "I scraped it against my locker today at school." Officer Donleavy became suspicious about Richard's reaction when asked him about what happened to his right hand.

"Oh really! Are you sure that didn't happen on Sarah Langston's face?" Richard became extremely belligerent as he continued to deny his involvement in Sarah's brutal beating once again.

"No officer, I didn't beat up anyone, especially my girlfriend, Sarah." Officer Donleavy immediately handcuffed Richard without hesitation. "Well...that's just what I want to find out for sure. I'm going to take you down to the station, just in case, because my report says otherwise. And Richard, I know what happened this morning at school in front of Sarah Langston's locker. We'll talk about it later at the station."

Officer Donleavy read Richard his Maranda rights.

"Richard Morris! You have the right to remain silent. Anything you say will be used against you in a court of law. You have the right to an attorney. If you cannot afford an attorney, one will be appointed for you. Do you understand your rights as I gave them to you, Richard Morris?"

Richard hands were cuffed while his parents stood and watched as his rights was read to him. Richard was immediately taken from their household. Richard answered to his rights.

"Yeah...yeah...I understand my rights."

Richard was placed in the back of Officer Donleavy's police cruiser. Eddie and Charlotte watched as their son was taken down to the police station for more questioning.

Chapter Six

"Sarah's Justice"

It was the late evening at the local hospital. The atmosphere in Sarah's hospital room after visiting hours was very quiet. It was just the way Sarah intended to be. Very quiet and peaceful. Sarah's nurse came to her room to check on her and to take her vital signs. Sarah was very depressed. She was very emotional. She muffled under her voice while she endured excruciating pain. The nurse asked Sarah how she felt.

"How are you doing, Sarah?"

Sarah responded to the nurse in tears.

"I'm in so much pain right now nurse. My face hurt really bad! I'm not so worried about myself right now. I'm so more worried about my baby...more than anything else right now. I'm wondering if my baby's okay!"

The nurse assured Sarah about her baby's condition. She was also curious to really know about what happened to Sarah and why she ended up in the hospital. Sarah had suffered slight memory lost from the brutal beating she took from Richard.

"Your baby is fine Sarah! There is nothing to worry about with the baby. We're continuously monitoring the baby every step of the way. We're also worrying about you as well. The nurse asked Sarah some questions. "If you don't mind me asking you Sarah? Do you know if your boyfriend did this to you? You got to remember, so that charges will be pressed against him."

"My boyfriend Richard! I don't know. He just…I don't know why he did this to me, when all I did was to let him and his parents know about the baby. That's it! Then the next morning…Richard threatened me because I embarrassed him in front of his parents. He said, I made him look like a wimp! That doesn't give Richard any reason to do what he did to me." Sarah cried out to the nurse. The nurse replied to Sarah.

"He had no call to do this to you. You don't need him, Sarah. Please get out before it's too late and before he comes after you again, because the next time he comes, he will kill you."

"That's what I'm saying! Oh my GOD!"

The nurse was very concerned for Sarah.

"Sarah…what is it? What is it?"

Sarah was scared and concerned for her safety and her life. Sarah began to hallucinate about Richard being present outside the hospital.

"He's still out there? Is he's going to kill me! Is he going to kill me! Sarah got out of her bed and looked out of the window of her hospital room, then back at the nurse. "Is he's still out there? Is he's going to get me? Is he going to hurt me? I know he will get me! It's a matter of time. It's a matter of time before Richard finds me and kills me!"

Sarah was immediately silent. She looked off from the nurse towards the window again. She wondered if Richard was lurking around outside with the intentions of coming up to her room to harm her. In Sarah's mind, Richard was still around and about… in her mind…Richard was lurking and haunting her in her imagination. That nurse requested counseling for Sarah during her long stay in the hospital.

It was the late evening at the police station. In the interrogation room, Richard was being interrogated by a Detective George Stevens and a Detective Robert Allen on the brutal assault and battery of his girlfriend Sarah. Richard sat facing the door in silence. Detective Stevens introduced himself as the lead detective George Stevens.

"I'm Detective George Stevens Richard...right there in front of you is Detective Robert Allen. I'm the lead detective in this investigation on the brutal assault and battery of your girlfriend, Sarah Langston."

Detective Stevens looked through his report on Richard Morris from the arresting Officer Donleavy. He was stunned about the brutality of Sarah's assault.

"It says here that Sarah Langston is your girlfriend, and it says here that she was brutally assaulted yesterday coming home from school. Did you brutally assault your girlfriend? You're going to tell me you don't know anything about this, do you, Richard?" Richard denied to the detectives that he had anything to do with Sarah's brutal beating. He continued acting as though nothing happened.

"Detective Stevens, I don't know what's going on here Richard. I don't know what you're trying to prove here."

Detective Stevens came closely into Richard's face, angered by Richard's comment. Detective Stevens came to a conclusion that Richard tried to manipulate the investigation.

"You don't know, Richard? You say you don't know what's going on?"

Detective Stevens fiercely paced the floor in anger.

"You'd better start thinking about where you're going to be in the next ten to twenty years to life if you don't start answering my questions, Richard."

Detective Robert Allen joined in with his line of questioning with Richard Morris. He aggressively questioned Richard. Detective Allen created a timeline to estimate what time Richard said he left school before Sarah was brutally attacked.

"What Detective Stevens is trying to ask you is what time did you leave school courtyard yesterday?"

Richard was reluctant to answer the detective directly.

"I don't really know when I left school, Detective Allen. I didn't look at no any time clock to know when I left."

Detective Stevens continued to look through his report on Richard. He was concerned about the time when Sarah left school courtyard and when Richard followed afterwards.

"According to your girlfriend, Sarah Langston's friends, Sarah left the school courtyard five to ten minutes after two o'clock after the last bell ranged. She was on her way home and given the estimated time, what time did you leave the school courtyard, Richard?" Detective Allen continued his aggressive line of question to Richard.

"About thirty minutes after that." Richard said he left school courtyard.

"I don't believe you about the time you left school, Richard. I have other witnesses say otherwise you left directly after the last bell rang, and that was exactly two o'clock when you and your two friends left the school grounds on the way home. I guess...and what I want to know is when did you and the other boys encounter Sarah Langston on your way home?"

Richard was fidgeting with his hands when he was questioned about him and his friends Kevin and Luther and when they encountered Sarah on their way home. Detective Stevens was very frustrated when he continued questioning Richard.

"No...we didn't see anyone! We didn't encounter anyone on the way home, Detective Stevens. My friends and I didn't encounter anyone on our way home."

Detective Stevens leaned over into Richard's face with intentions of getting the truth from him.

"You're lying to me, Richard. I am going to get the truth even if it takes all night long. Now...who were the other boys with you?"

Richard refused to give up his friends' identities.

"I'm not telling you jack...crap-olla." Richard yelled out to the two detectives.

Detective Allen abruptly grabbed the right side of Richard's head and slammed it onto the table in haste when Richard refused to cooperate with the detective's line of questioning. Detective Stevens looked on.

"You'd better start answering the questions that Detective Stevens asked you, because we're tired of playing these stupid games that you're concoct in your stupid little pea brain head. Give the detective what he wants to hear. He's tired of playing with you. I'm tired of playing. Now, answer his questions, you scum bag."

Detective Stevens leaned over into Richard's face once again while his head was glued with Detective Allen's hand still clamped to his face on the table.

"Yes...Detective Allen is right! I'm tired of playing with scum like you who doesn't want to cooperate with me, and all I'm trying to do is help you. It makes me so angry with a creature like you, who keeps lying to me about beating a helpless young woman, and she's pregnant too. I hate she polluted her gene pool with your semen, but it's not the baby's fault. It's like you're beating that poor little baby inside her womb too. When I hear things like that and see it, it makes me sick to my stomach, Richard. Now, I want you... knuckle head...tell me what I want to know."

Richard gave up his friends Kevin Osborne and Luther Rollins instead, while his interrogation was still in process.

"I'm not saying another word, but I will give you Kevin Osborne and Luther Rollins."

Richard never admitted or even confessed to Sarah's brutal beating. He was hand cuffed and transported to a holding cell by Detective Allen.

"Thank you, Cain! Detective Allen...put this scum bag in lock up until further notice."

Richard was transported out of the interrogation room by Detective Allen, kicking and screaming and shouting and yelling out to Detective Stevens.

"Hey, I didn't beat up anyone. I didn't touch my girlfriend! I didn't do anything! Why are you holding me?"

Detective Allen transported Richard aggressively to the holding cell.

"Shut up…shut up…before I use force and beat the living tar out of you."

Detective Stevens called for officers that who were out on location to pick up Kevin Osborne and Luther Rollins for questioning in the brutal attack of Sarah Langston.

Meanwhile, at the Morris's household, the evening was later than usual. Eddie and Charlotte Morris were very frustrated about their son's innuendoes and his trouble with the law. They both came to a solution about their son's future. Eddie fiercely paced the floor in the foyer.

"I'm so tired of trying to help that boy, Charlotte. We tried to help Richard in every way possible. We tried to keep him on the right path. Not this time! For brutally attacking Sarah. Richard will never abide by any of the rules that we provide for him. Eddie was completely giving up on Richard. We got to do something, Charlotte. Richard needs to go somewhere!"

"What are you suggesting, Eddie? Charlotte said. "What are we going to do with Richard?"

Eddie came to a solution about Richard's future and where to place him.

"Richard need to get out of our house…right now. If he can't abide by what we tell him around here, Charlotte and follow the guidelines we provide him in order to put him on the right path, then it's time for him to leave this wonderful castle, Charlotte. We're not his royal care givers anymore" Charlotte replied with ultimatum in Richard's fate.

"God only knows, Eddie, we both tried to raise our child the best possible way we knew how. He doesn't want to listen to us anymore, so Eddie, as of right now, I agree with you. Richard has to go!"

Eddie and Charlotte expressed their true emotions about their son, Richard. Eddie decides Richard fate.

"If our son is convicted of that brutal crime against Sarah, at least he'll have a home made of concrete and bars, bare mattresses and pillows. He can't come back here...unless he can abide by our rules. I have no other alternatives for Richard at this point. I love our son, Charlotte. I love him very much, but...there is one thing we can give Richard and that's tough love. I'm going to give him that until he learns the realities of a life."

Charlotte felt guilty about what happened to Sarah. She was reminded repeatedly about her brutal attack.

"I can't believe our son. Why did this happen to Sarah? Why? And for what reason did Richard have to attack that girl, Eddie?" Charlotte said is disbelief. Eddie responds to Charlotte.

"He doesn't want to be responsible for himself, or take responsibility for that little baby inside Sarah. I think that is why our son brutally beat Sarah. I don't know what to do, or what to say about Richard anymore, Charlotte. I just don't know anymore."

Eddie stood in the foyer of his house in a complete daze. He was staring at Charlotte. He felt very disappointed about his Richard's indiscretions. He decided to let go of Richard he once knew as son, Richard. Eddie and Charlotte gave up on Richard to the State for their benefit until he learns to abide by their rules and regulations at home.

It was the early morning hours at the police station. Kevin Osborne and Luther Rollins were brought into the interrogation room by two of the arresting officers. Detective Stevens interrogated Kevin Osborne first for the brutal beating of Sarah Langston. The detectives introduce themselves to Richard's friend Luther Rollins.

"I'm Detective George Stevens and I'm the lead detective on this case. On your right is Detective Robert Allen. We're investigating the brutal assault of Sarah Langston. Sarah was beaten brutally to a pulp about the face by her boyfriend, Richard Morris, your so called friend, the scum bag." Detective Stevens start his line of question with Kevin Osborne. "I want you to tell me about what you know about Richard and why this girl, Sarah Langston was beaten to a pulp brutally in the face by that scum bag, Richard Morris." Kevin didn't waste any time answering the detective questions.

"All I know...when Luther Rollins, Richard Morris and I was walking home from school, we all spotted Richard's girlfriend, Sarah Langston, walking home from school. Richard decided to go over and talk to her about something. That's all I know, Detective Stevens!"

Detective Stevens looked through his report.

"What time did you all leave the school grounds before you all encountered Sarah Langston?" Detective Stevens asked Kevin.

"We all left just after two o'clock...right after the last bell ring to go home." Kevin replied to the detective.

"What were Richard and your other friend, Luther Rollins, doing when you were all on your way home from school?" Detective Stevens asked Kevin.

"Richard was talking a lot about Sarah. I don't remember what all he was saying. I was busy doing something else at the time." Kevin replied.

"Can you give a brief timeline of the events when you, Luther Rollins, and Richard Morris encountered Sarah Langston right after you all left school. How many minutes? Give me a rough estimate?"

"A good ten minutes or so, Detective Stevens. I'm telling you! I'm not going to jail for Richard. That cat is crazy in a whole lot of ways kid!" Kevin gave up Richard. He told the truth about Richard intentions on hurting Sarah. Detective Stevens escorted Kevin into the next interrogation room before he bought, his and Richards friend, Luther Rollins in to be interrogated.

"Kevin...what I'm going to do is have you escorted to another room right now until further notice. I need to speak to your friend, Luther Rollins."

Detective Stevens leaned over into Kevin's face with the intentions of receiving the truth from him when further questioned about the case.

"I will be talking to you again. You don't mind if I talk to your friend, Luther do you?"

"Go for it sir, I don't have nothing to hide."

Detective Allen transported Kevin to the next interrogation room…room number two. The detective was still in disbelief about Kevin's story of what really happened when Sarah Langston was brutally attacked.

"I think you do, Kevin. I still think you do have something to hide. You're going to tell me more about Richard and what his attitude was like when he encountered his girlfriend, Sarah. Detective Stevens is going to give you some time to come up with some more beef on your friend, Richard Morris and what you're still hiding from us."

Detective Allen transported Kevin to Interrogation Room two for further notice. Luther Rollins was brought into interrogation room number one to be interrogated by Detective Stevens.

"I'm Detective Stevens. I'm investigating the brutal assault of Sarah Langston. I think you know why you're here, Luther. I don't want to joke around with this mess anymore, because I'm tired and I'm sleepy. I like to go home and get some rest. Detective Stevens leaned over into Luther's face.

"Tell me what I want to know, Luther." Luther responded to the detective.

"What do you want to know, Detective Stevens? I didn't do anything."

Detective Stevens became more and more frustrated. He was belligerent with Luther. He slammed the table over against the wall, which triggered a domino effect. He gained the attention of the entire police station.

"That's what I'm talking about! You guys never do anything wrong, or think you do anything wrong. Give me what I want, knuckle head! I'll ask you this question. What time did you leave from school yesterday? What time and don't lie?"

"A little bit after two o'clock, Detective Stevens. Richard Morris, Kevin Osborne, and I were walking home from school courtyard. Along the way, we met up with Richard's girlfriend, Sarah. Richard called out to her. He wanted to talk to her about something." Luther replied to the detective.

"What did Richard want to discuss with Sarah? What was his attitude at that particular time towards her?"

"I tell you, Detective Stevens, it was like Sodom and Gomorrah in Genesis time. He was so angry with Sarah about something. He ran up to her and he stopped her. Richard wanted to talk to her about something. I don't know what! I promise detective, I don't know what it was Richard wanted to talk about to his girlfriend, Sarah."

Detective Allen returned with Kevin Osborne. Kevin wanted to confess to Detective Stevens about what he heard Richard tell Sarah when they encountered her.

"Detective Stevens…I'm sorry to disturb your interrogation and questioning of Luther Rollins. Our friend, Kevin has something he wants to talk about, and he insists that he do it in here with you and Luther. I think he's had a little time to reflect on what it would be like to stay here and all the accommodations that comes with it. Think that our friend was thinking of All he could think the freshly painted cells, the dirty mattresses, the pillows with no pillow cases on them, an open toilet, and trying a cell on for size. Our friend Kevin wants to talk now…if you please?"

Luther looked over at Kevin coming into the interrogation room. He was nervous about what Kevin was going to tell the detective. Luther decides to change his story and confess as well. Detective Stevens paces the interrogation room in desperation of what Kevin was going to reveal.

"Well…well…well…. Mr. Osborne, it is very nice to see you again, son. Are you ready to talk son, or you're going to tell me more lies? Tell me what you really know about Richard Morris and what he told Sarah Langston when he confronted her."

Kevin was very nervous about what Richard would find out what he and Luther told the police. He confessed to the Detective Stevens about Richard's state of mind.

"I'm not going to jail for Richard. Kevin encouraged Luther to tell the true. Kevin told the detective about what happened to Sarah."

Detective Allen convinced Kevin to confess to Richard's state of mind and about what happened when Sarah was brutally attacked.

"Shoot…you would want to tell the detective about what happen and just maybe you want to share a cell with Richard for eternity, because he has one ready for him as we speak. Tell the detective everything he wants to know. Go Kevin…shoot!"

Kevin was very nervous about the facts of the case and about Richard finding out he and Luther gave him up to the police. Kevin told Detective Allen his side of the story using his flash back in a chain of event surrounding Sarah's brutal attack and Richard indiscretions. Kevin began experiencing flash backs about Richard and about how he was talking about Sarah horribly.

"Richard…he's like crazy as a tick sometimes. He is as evil as some people come in this lifetime. We're walking home from school. Kevin continued to give commentary of the moments leading to Sarah's brutal assault. I overheard Richard as talked about what he was going to do to Sarah.

She shouldn't have embarrassed him like that in front of his parents. He said, she made me look like an idiot. Richard said, his father Eddie beat him moments after Sarah and her father left his house. Richard wanted to give Sarah what his father gave to him. A good behind butt whipping! He wanted to disfigure and rearrange Sarah's face, beat it to a pulp. He wanted the power to own her at that particular moment. He wanted to make it so that no one else could have her. He wanted to understand how he felt when I got that beaten down by father, Eddie."

Kevin's flash backs ended with Richard threatening Sarah and what he was going to do to her. Kevin confessed to the detectives the cruel things Richard said about Sarah to the Detectives. Before Kevin could finish confessing, Luther interrupted Kevin while he was confessing to the detectives.

"Richard was saying some things about Sarah that made me quiver. He said that she embarrassed him in front of his parents about her being pregnant with his baby and other things he never disclosed about what happened. He said that he felt humiliated, and he looked like an idiot when got beaten down by his daddy."

Immediately, …Kevin interrupted while Luther was in the middle of confessing.

"This was all because of Sarah told his parents that she was pregnant with his baby. He beat that girl like flies on a piece of meat. She was a piece of garbage at that point. He punched Sarah all in her face. All I could see were his arms and elbows."

Kevin was nervous. He interrupted Luther's confession again as he confessed to the detectives.

"He beat that girl like he stole something out of a pawn shop. Sarah didn't deserve that at all, because it was normal…like when you get news about a pregnancy. He's a total freak and a coward. He couldn't confess it himself. She confessed, and he beat her brutally for it."

Luther continued to tell more to the detective's about Richard's attitude and disposition and what he was like as he explained earlier when he was interrogated at the beginning.

"Like I said, Richard's attitude was like Sodom and Gomorrah. Nothing good came out of it, or from it, or out of it, you know what I'm saying to you?"

Detective Stevens was very thankful to Kevin and Luther for their truthful confessions of what happened during a trail of events that occurred during the time that when Sarah Langston walked home from school.

"I'm glad that you both decided to confess to this thing. I thought I was going to be here for the rest of the morning and miss out on some much needed sleep. I really appreciate your confessing up and coming clean about this case against Richard Morris. He now belongs to us, the State. Thanks for your cooperation, boys."

Detective Allen released Kevin and Luther out of custody.

"You both can breathe right now. Bye! You'll both be escorted out the front door. Thanks boys."

Both Kevin and Luther were very relieved about they're their confession to Sarah's brutal assault. Their confession was a very positive for Sarah in her defense. Detective Stevens and Detective Allen gave commentary towards the facts that Richard Morris lied about the attack on his girlfriend, Sarah Langston, and their unborn child. Detective Stevens was very discussed about being lied to.

"Richard Morris...that scum bag lied to us about his involvement with the assault on his girlfriend, Sarah Langston. Detective Allen...I even saw the fresh scar marks on his right hand. I didn't want to ask him about it. I should've asked about it, but... to tell you the truth, I knew he beat that girl to a pulp with that dag gum. That fresh scar mark was more than proof. I didn't want to spook him; I knew he would start spinning webs all over the place."

"So, take another approach. Let's do like we did with the other two weirdos, Detective Stevens. I think it's about time to we get his friends to confess openly and truthfully to Richard's assault on his girlfriend and their unborn child. I feel so sorry for the girl and that poor little baby for having a dirt bag like that."

"You got it, Detective Allen! Now, let's go and arrest that knuckle head so I can go home and get some sleep...Jesus Christ!"

Both Detective Stevens and Detective Allen left the interrogation room number one. They proceeded towards the holding cell where Richard was stashed. They arrested and charged him with the assault and battery of Sarah Langston and with the intent to harm her unborn child. Justice was served for Sarah and her unborn child as time went on. The trial and the sentencing of Richard Morris had commenced. Richard was accused of brutal assault and battery on his girlfriend, Sarah and the attempt to harm their unborn child. He was to spend twenty years to life in prison.

Chapter Seven

"A Blessing for Sarah"

It was the early afternoon. Sarah recovered from her injuries, although her self confidence and her self esteem was deeply destroyed. She became emotionally impaired. Her black eyes, busted lip, and her black and blue bruises on her body reminded her of the attack. Sarah's friends, Emily and Denise came over to the Langston household for a visit. Paul Langston welcomed the girls into his home. Emily entered through the door first. She saw Sarah was sitting on the sofa. Emily noticed Sarah's bruised face when she walked into the living room. Sarah became emotional when she saw Emily. She started to cry.

"Sarah...I'm not going to ask how are. By the looks of your face, it displays a very sad story. "Oh my God, Sarah, you look like you're in excruciating pain!" Denise entered the living room. She also noticed Sarah's bruised face from a distance from the doorway.

Denise was becoming startled and very emotional. She was also in tears. Denise expressed her feelings about Richard.

"OH...MY GOD! That monster! That scumbag! Sarah... look at your face! All because you told his parents about your pregnancy."

Sarah was feeling depressed and guilty about what had happened to her. She downed herself with pity while in the presence of Emily and Denise.

"You both tried to tell me. How could I be so stupid! I was just so stupid! You both told me what Richard was capable of. I didn't want to listen to you both, or take heed to what you both were telling me. I thought I knew Richard, I thought I could change him...with the baby and all. I almost paid the ultimate price for not listening...with my face. I thank God he didn't harm our baby."

Emily was still feeling guilty for not walking home with Sarah before her brutal attack occurred. She expressed her thoughts to Sarah about Richard and the guilt she felt about not taking heed to her first reactions of what to do when she knew her friend was in trouble.

"Sarah...after he threatened you that day at the lockers, I should have done something. I was very scared and afraid for you, but I didn't take heed to my first intentions of Richard. Denise and I were supposed to walk home with you that day, but...we didn't. I'm going to always feel guilty for that, Sarah."

Denise also expressed her guilt to Sarah.

"I'm so sorry for not walking with you, Sarah. We shouldn't have listened to you when you said that you were fine. Sarah...you weren't okay! It was our intuitions to follow you home when we felt that something wasn't right with Richard."

"I understand, Emily...Denise. I really do understand now! It would have saved me from that brutal beating from Richard and a lot of pain."

The girls shared a group hug with all the trimmings. They put all of the chaos and the bad memories of Richard behind them. Sarah continued to be relieved about the fact that Richard will never hurt her, or the baby again. Sarah was visited by the Morris's. They were there at the Langston household to apologize for their son, Richard indiscretions and the brutal assault on Sarah. Eddie and Charlotte wanted to try to heal old wounds from the tragedy that hit their families so hard. Eddie Morris and his wife, Charlotte didn't know whether they would be welcomed in the Langston household. They started to turn and walk away without looking back at the Langston household. Eddie and Charlotte decided to chance in their fate and visit the Langston's. Their thoughts of being rejected by Paul Langston was held in high regards, especially when it came to their son Richard and all the chaos he has caused for brutalizing and assaulting his daughter, Sarah. Paul answered the door without haste towards the Morris's...although he was still upset for what Richard did to his daughter, Sarah. Eddie apologized to Paul at the entrance of the front door with Charlotte alongside him. Paul agreed to hear Eddie out.

"Hello, Mr. Langston! I know by now that you don't want our acquaintance at your residence, but Charlotte and I came to apologize to you, especially to your daughter, Sarah for our son, Richard indiscretions and the brutal assault on your daughter, Sarah. Paul encouraged Sarah to come into the living room and visit with the Morris's. "Sarah...if you don't mind...can we come in to visit with you, please?"

Paul offered Eddie and Charlotte a seat in the living room without any hard feelings towards them about their son's indiscretions.

"Please come in. Welcome to my home. I'm a reasonable man, Eddie. There are no hard feelings against you, or your wife Charlotte. Welcome to the Langston household. Would you both care for a cold drink? Please...come in and sit down in the living room, if you may."

"No thank you, Mr. Langston. Nothing to drink for us. We just came to apologize to you and to your daughter Sarah for everything my son, Richard has put you through. First of all, I would like to say personally, I'm sorry for what happened to your daughter, Sarah.

We're both very sorry for what happened to Sarah and our unborn grandbaby. We can't begin to imagine Sarah's pain and what she suffered and your pain as well. Eddie asked Paul for permission for him and Charlotte to see Sarah. Paul proudly gave permission to Eddie and Charlotte to see his daughter, Sarah. "Is it alright, Paul, if we can see your daughter, Sarah?"

"It's alright, Eddie and Charlotte!"

Eddie continued feeling guilty about what happened to Sarah. He expressed his deepest feelings to about his son, Richard to Paul.

"Mr. Langston! Charlotte and I tried so hard with Richard! We tried so hard! Richard is a totally different person to us now. Charlotte and I has given up on our Richard in a whole lot of ways. We still love our son, no matter what."

Charlotte decided her son fate. She put the icing on the cake... ending a chapter with Richard. There was no ending to the story behind it. She expressed her deepest love her son Richard to Paul.

"Like Eddie said, Paul...Eddie and I tried with Richard. He would not abide by our rules and regulations according to our home. Since the brutal beating of your daughter, Sarah...Eddie and I put our son, Richard out of our home. His home is now the state jail." Paul gave Eddie and Charlotte words of advice.

"When a child like that is disobedient to the fact and you feel he do not want to take heed to what you or your husband say or do for him, or what is done for him...what else can you do about a child who do not listen to reason? You let them go just as you see fit! You had to Richard go! He need to what it is to experience a world without you both in it. Give him a little taste of how hard life can be for him. "Tough love is what I call it!" Maybe Richard will decide to straighten up. Believe me! Just maybe he will."

Eddie was very thankful to Paul for the advice he gave. He figured in a way that he and Charlotte could fully understand about their son, Richard indiscretions. They felt more welcomed in the Langston household. There were no hard feelings were felt between their two families. Paul called out for Sarah.

"Sarah, …sweetie, …the Morris's are here to see you." Sarah came downstairs to visit with the Morris's Charlotte noticed Sarah's bruised face and revealing parts of her body. She became very emotional after seeing Sarah. She knew the damage was done to Sarah by her son, Richard.

"Oh my God …Sarah! What did my son do to you? Oh baby… I'm so sorry."

Charlotte turned to Eddie and embraced him in disbelief of Sarah's appearance. Eddie also noticed Sarah's bruised face. He was also emotional. Charlotte had never in all her days of marriage to Eddie, seen him cry. She was very surprised and shocked. The Morris's emotions were very understandable. Eddie immediately apologized to Sarah.

"I'm so sorry, Sarah for my son, Richard. Saddened, discussed and disappointed about what their son, Richard's indiscretions. Eddie continued to embrace Charlotte before leaving the Langston household. Eddie and Charlotte couldn't look at Sarah without feeling guilty, because of the magnitude of her injuries. Eddie and Charlotte prepared themselves to leave the Langston household. Paul opened the front door for Eddie and Charlotte. They left without uttering another word. Sarah understood why the Morris's exited the house.

"I know that the Morris's meant well. I'm not mad with them at all, daddy. I feel a little peace! It's not my baby's fault that he or she is inside me. All I know is that I'm going to love my baby, no matter what with all of my heart. Sarah embraced her father. "I love you, daddy!"

Paul gave into his emotions as embraced his daughter. With all the events that occurred throughout the months past, the Langston household was full of love and happiness…even for a brief moment. Paul expressed that unconditional love for Sarah and his unborn grandchild.

"I love you, Sarah…more than my life. The day you hold your child in your arms, you're going to know what it feels like to love and love unconditionally. Your child…my grandchild will bring you a lot of joy and happiness. He or she will mean the world to you as you do me. Emily and Denise joined Paul and Sarah Langston in a group hug filled moment with a lot of love and understanding. It was a very special way to end a perfect day. Six months later after Sarah's brutal assault, she was fully recovered. Within the days after her recovery, Sarah Langston gave birth to a healthy 7 pounds 5 ounces' baby boy. She named him,

"Paul Robert Langston."

THE END

Printed in the United States
By Bookmasters